TERROR IN RIO

Terror in Rio

Alan Caillou

NEW ENGLISH LIBRARY
TIMES MIRROR

First published in the United States of America by Pinnacle Books, June 1971
Copyright © Pinnacle Books 1971

*

FIRST NEL PAPERBACK EDITION OCTOBER 1973

*

NEL Books are published by
New English Library Limited from Barnard's Inn, Holborn, London, E. C. 1
Made and printed in Great Britain by Hunt Barnard Printing Ltd., Aylesbury, Bucks.

45001637 4

CHAPTER ONE

TAPAJOS, AMAZON.
Co-ordinates: 5.87S: 56.12W.

How could a man run so fast when the *Ilianas* were tangling themselves around his feet, reaching out, it seemed, to find his ankles and wrap their tentacles around them, sending him sprawling to the ground, face down in the slimy black humus, every time he thrust his body forward?

How could he force his way so stubbornly through the dark jungle, faster even than the *pium* flies that were a cloud of venomous pain around his head?

He knew how; it was the fear.

The giant casuarina trees kept out the sun, with bright red orchids like pinpoints of luminescent fire among them. But this was not cool shade, it was the steamy, fetid heat that he'd only read about, heard about in the lectures Rick Meyers had given before this operation started, with the air around him – what there was of it – the air of a baker's oven. The mimosas towered around him, and even the ferns were twenty feet above his head. He felt like an ant forcing his laborious way over the ground, driven on by fear and the smell of blood.

And behind him, *they* were coming, coming up fast, in a silence that was uncanny. He could hear his own footsteps, squelching through the mud, rustling the fallen leaves in the dry patches, cracking the broken, rotting branches underfoot, and splashing through sudden, unexpected patches of clear water. And yet, behind him . . . *How can they move so silently?* he was thinking.

He used the machete, slashing savagely at the vines, wishing incongruously, as though that were all he had to worry about, that he had a stone on which to sharpen its blunted edge, knowing that soon he would be using it for other purposes too, cutting into bodies if he didn't stay ahead of them. Or would they get close enough to him for the hand-to-hand combat he knew so well, had been trained in so expertly? Perhaps not; they had their deadly little bows; they would keep their distance. And his own great strength would help him not at all if they wouldn't come within fifty feet of him.

He forced himself on, urging his gaunt, exhausted, body forward, pace by pace, knowing there could be no relief and that he would simply have to run until he dropped.

The forest opened up, just a trifle, and there was tall, yellow pampas grass with a wide stream running through it, and he splashed through the water and reached the other bank, and crawled under a fallen tree that blocked his way, dragging himself painfully through the mud among long sharp thorns that ripped at his bleeding skin. He felt the bite of a leech on his thigh, and brushed it off savagely, and clambered on to a sandbar where the stinging insects were a thick black cloud that wrapped themselves around his head again and smothered him; he could not believe there could be so many of them. They were smaller than mosquitoes, the *pium* flies, and they hung in the air in great dark masses over the sandbars; their millions of thin bites could kill a peccary. The natives kept well out of their way, keeping clear of the sandbanks that were the *pium*'s home.

He splashed onward and found the sheltering, sweating trees again, and he heard them clearly now as they took to the water behind him, making a little detour to clear the bar. Were there *piranas* there, he wondered?

Another clearing, and he almost pulled up short in alarm; there was a wide, open space here, a band of bright green moss that half-circled the jungle he had come from, a broad crescent more than three hundred yards across, a concave arch with the nearest cover a little to one side; a hundred and eighty yards, he calculated. He looked back wildly and saw them, and prayed for strength for a burst of animal speed.

The moss was soft and resilient under his feet as he raced across it, his feet making wide, steaming depressions. He could hear the pounding of his own heart, and the stitch in his lungs was unbearable.

He thought of Heinneman – how long had it taken him to die? – and forced himself on.

The moss was softer, and he knew with sudden terror that there was quicksand under it; he shortened his stride and seemed to dance on it, and fell when it gave way under his feet and he looked back again to see them, quite clearly now, a hundred yards behind him, treading the moss lightly, carefully, knowing its dangers. There were four of them, with one of them – was it

Leros? – well out in the lead, the others streaking over the green surface to cover the flanks. Leros was carrying a bow, slight and short and useless-looking, but quite deadly; there was strychnine on the arrowheads, and all that was needed was a scratch, just enough to draw blood. One had a rifle, a modern Garand, but he knew there were no bullets left in it. The others carried the long *facaos*, the jungle knife with which they could disembowel a man in two or three quick and easy slashes, so fast you could hardly see the movement of the blade; he'd seen them carve Heinneman up like that, and the memory of it made him shudder and forced him on.

How long could he keep going?

Not for me the quick death, he was thinking. *They want me alive, in fear and in pain, but alive, the tongue to talk with before it's sliced off, the hands to pray with before they are amputated.*

The trees were still a long way off. Struggling forward, he looked back. Leros was on one knee now, drawing his bow, and he threw himself into the moss and heard the arrow whistle over his head. For a moment, he hesitated, knowing that further flight was useless, wondering if he could charge into them with his machete . . .

He ran instead towards the trees, his legs pumping mechanically, all hope gone and only the willpower driving him. He thought, with a sudden touch of callous humor – they told us in the school, Col. Tobin's private school for his Private Army, that you keep on moving no matter what, every minute you earn may just be the moment of your salvation . . .

That Rick Meyers! That lecturer! He should be here now, he was thinking . . .

Ahead of him there was the silent, awesome, immensity of the jungle again; if he could reach the trees once more . . .

And then the shot rang out, almost directly ahead of him, quite close, the marksman on the edge of the forest. There was a second shot, and a third, and then, after the briefest of pauses, a fourth; he did not hear the bullets. He flopped to the ground and gave up, letting the sense of helplessness seep over him, letting things take their own course now, knowing that he could go no further, could think no longer, could do nothing but resign himself to whatever was in store for him.

'You never give up,' Rick had said, 'you keep on going whatever the odds, because the odds change sometimes, and you're going to be sore if they change just a moment after you laid yourself down and died . . . ' He had a strange, sardonic wit, Rick

7

Meyers; had he ever known this kind of terror? The slime was pressing into his face, and he dragged himself to his feet and staggered to the nearest tree, and draped himself over its lower branches, his long arms hanging down, the chest pumping hard to fill itself with air.

Then suddenly, Leros was stretched out on the bright green carpet that was already stained with his blood. One of the others, a little way behind him, was squatting, it seemed, in a patch of yellow weed, slowly sinking, motionless, into the sand below it; it seemed incredible that he could sit like that and be dead. The crumpled form of another lay to one side, and the last man, the big *mestizo*, the one with the rifle and no bullets left for it, was draped on his back over a grey-blue rock. Even at this distance, he could see the small black hole in the center of the forehead.

He began to laugh, almost hysterically, and then he heard Paul's voice, loud and clear and very calm: 'Over here, Edgars. Keep under cover. Take it easy, there might be more of them. But you're covered.'

For a long time he hung on his branch, wanting to pull himself together before he should answer the summons; he was ashamed of the hysteria, of the fear; he wondered if the Major would be mad at him. He began to walk slowly in the direction the voice had come from, along the edge of the jungle, and in a moment he saw Paul Tobin drop down lightly from the tree he had been using, the rifle still ready, and he said quietly: 'Just the four of them, Paul. Just four.'

Paul was not looking at him; those restless, intelligent eyes were searching the other side of the swamp. 'Are you sure?'

'I'm sure. That was pretty fancy shooting.'

Paul lowered the rifle. He shrugged. 'They were sitting ducks. Where's Heinneman?'

'Heinneman's dead.'

The freckled, boyish face was hard. There was no cannon fodder in the Private Army; the loss of one man was hard to take, the way it should be.

Edgars said: 'Man, I don't scare easy, I guess you know that, but . . . back there, I was scared. They had us both staked out on the ground, and they slashed open his belly and flicked the guts out like it was . . . you know the way you unravel a sock? Jesus, I never knew a man had so much gut inside him. A fellow called Leros did it.' He pointed. 'That one, there.'

Paul was holding out a flask, and Edgars took it and drank

8

gratefully, and said: 'Irish whiskey, kinda makes me feel . . . at home again.' He shuddered. 'I never knew a man could live so long with his guts spread out all over the place, never knew a man could scream so much.'

He took another long drink, and said: 'The Colonel's private stock. In the middle of the Brazilian jungle you run into a guy drinking Irish whiskey, and you know what? You know that help's at hand, and the Old Man ain't far off. It's a comfort, Paul, I can tell you. A real comfort.'

It felt as though the breath would never return to his body.

Paul said: 'Did you get it?'

Edgars' coal-black face was shining with sweat, pure ebony. He said with a twisted smile: 'Take a guess, Major.'

'Good, good. We've got a camp ahead, two miles, and Rick owes me a thousand *cruzeiros.*'

'Huh?'

'He bet me you wouldn't make it, he figured the odds were too high.'

'That Rick. He's a computer, always figuring . . . ' He broke off and said again: 'Christ, I was scared. You ever been scared like that?'

'Oh yes. Often.'

'I'm a street-fighter, Paul, I got to have walls around me, burning automobiles, fuzz in gas masks, kids waving placards, guys sniping at me from roof-tops . . . '

'You did pretty well in Vietnam.'

'Yeah, so they tell me. I did better when I got back to Chicago. A man can't fight the way he should when he's ten thousand miles from home.'

'When the time comes, there just might be plenty of that too, in Rio. Bramble says it looks pretty bad.'

Edgars held out his hand for the flask again, and Paul passed it over and watched him drink. He said: 'Where is it?'

Edgars screwed the top back on to the thin silver flask and gestured with it: 'Back there, about four miles I guess, hidden in a tree, inside my water bottle. Ain't nobody gonna find it, ever.' A toucan was peering at them from a branch close by, inquisitive, its head jerking this way and that; it made up its mind and squawked at them loudly and Edgars said: 'You too, Charlie.' He looked at Paul and said: 'They're pretty good to eat, did you know that?'

The heat was impossible, the steam rising up out of the ground and enveloping them.

Edgars said: 'Back there, three or four miles, they started to catch up with me, so I figured I'd better get rid of it. Not that it would have done much good. Just a matter of principle. I figured I might persuade them I'd passed it on to someone else, given them something to worry about.'

Paul was laughing quietly. Edgars said: 'I can find it easy enough if you want it. But I memorised it. Wasn't hard, once I figured out the handwriting.'

A shadow of doubt passed over Paul's young face, and Edgars caught the trend of his thoughts and said: 'Yeah, yeah, I know what you mean, a foreign language. But don't sell the school short, Paul, they're pretty damn good. Sure, they never quite got my accent right, but reading . . . I'm pretty damn good at it. Seven names, and the rest . . . it wasn't hard.'

'Give me the names first.'

Edgars said promptly: 'Cheleiros, Arrifana, Santarem, Ajuda, Alacrimo, Juliao, and Xira.'

'And you're absolutely sure of them . . . '

'You want it backwards?' The toucan was peering at them again, coming in closer, hesitant but unafraid. Edgars said: 'Xira, Juliao, Alacrimo, Ajuda, Santarem, Arrifana and Cheleiros. You want the rest in Portuguese, or in English?'

'First in English. Sit down, make yourself comfortable.' Edgars sat down heavily on the trunk of a fallen tree and began to recite: '*Xira to Santarem. I have decided to take your advice on the matter of the Indians. As you say, we do not need them except in their capacity as fodder for the Brazilian troops . . .* '

Paul said sharply: 'Fodder?'

'*Carne de cannao*, I make that cannon fodder.'

'Right. Go on.'

' . . . *and therefore we will place our whole reliance on a feint . . .* '

'*Fingimento?*'

'Yes. *A feint by your mestizos, followed by an assault when the fodder has been consumed*, no, *will have been consumed*, it was the future subjunctive, *and the enemy thereby considerably weakened. I am sending you Alacrimo to command the Indians. He knows what to do. Arrifana, of course, must stay at his office, and I need Juliao and Ajuda still, at least until the sabotage programme is stabilised. In the matter of Cheleiros, my suspicions might, as you suggest, be groundless, but in any case, she has outlived her usefulness, and I have therefore ordered her*

10

execution. Long live the New Revolution, Death to all our Enemies.'

Paul was frowning darkly. He said: 'Let me have it in Portuguese,' and Edgars slowly, hesitantly, repeated it. When he had finished, Paul was pacing restlessly, his rifle held by the barrel, with its stock slung over his shoulder. The shadows were lengthening, the jungle sounds of the early evening starting up as the howler monkeys came out and began their ceaseless search for insects; the sun hurt their eyes, and they always waited till it was low in the sky, spending the daylight hours in the hidden recesses of their lairs; like the *mestizo* army they were hunting, Paul was thinking.

He stopped his pacing and said: 'We know some of those names, don't we? On the others . . . we'd better do a little research. Do you get the impression that Cheleiros is in Rio?'

Edgars nodded. 'I'd say so. That's where Xira is, and if he was sending an order for her execution up here, he'd have worded it different.'

'Yes, I think so.'

'You know who she is?'

Paul shook his head. 'We soon will. I wonder . . . Yes, that just might make some sort of sense. How many men in their camp?'

'Give or take a couple, six hundred. Mostly *mestizos,* about fifty, sixty of them, honkies . . . ' He grinned quickly. 'By my standards, not by yours. The rest, Indians. A lot of machine guns, Paul, I'd say at least two hundred, the *mestizos* were teaching some of the Indians how to use them. Some of them seemed to know already. Four big crates of rifles came in while we were there, the German K43 carbine, 7.92mm., that's a pretty good gun. The cases had shipping tags on them – *Ixiamas.* Don't ask me where that is.'

'It's in Bolivia, an up-country army camp.'

Edgars frowned. 'Bolivia? Why should the Bolivians support a movement like the Xiristas?'

'They're reaching out,' Paul said, 'taking help from wherever they can get it. In the towns, up-river, even over the border . . . '

It was a point that the Colonel, Paul's father, had made back in London, when the Minister, in great secrecy, had first approached him for help from the Private Army. Colonel Tobin had said, lecturing, sure of his own expertise: 'This is what Che Guevara and Regis Debray were squabbling about, did you know that? One said that revolutions were fought in the hills, the other insisted that the towns provided more fertile fields. And

11

your Juan Xira has combined both those philosophies, the urban and the buccolic. He started as a simple terrorist, and when he found he commanded an army of violent criminals, he decided to take over the whole country, that's the kind of man he is. He began by raiding upcountry army posts for weapons, and now . . . now, every bandit and outlaw from the wild lands of the Amazon is flocking to him . . . You've got a major war on your hands, Minister.'

The Minister had thrown up his arms, gesticulating feverishly. 'That's why I come to you, Colonel. In their jungle hide-outs, the Xirista army is simply . . . simply better than we are. Our Government forces have taken appalling losses, and in the towns, yes, the towns too . . . foreign diplomats have been kidnapped, officials murdered, a programme of applied terror that has simply grown beyond our means to counter. We need your help, Colonel Tobin. Regardless of cost, if we are to save our country from yet another wave of terror . . . we *must* have it.'

Colonel Tobin said gently: 'My Private Army, Minister, is the smallest, the toughest, the most efficient in the world. But if I'm to stamp out a revolution, I need a free hand. Carte blanche. To fight it in my own way, with no interference from you or anybody else.'

The heavy load was slipping off the minister's shoulders; but he wanted to hold on to the reins. He said: 'All the military help you need, we will supply . . . ' and the Colonel interrupted him brusquely and said:

'No sir. We act alone, and in secret.'

'But . . . but surely . . . '

The Colonel said dryly: 'The continuing success of my Private Army hinges on two things. First, we put out brush fires before they get out of hand. Secondly, we operate with the tacit – the *very* tacit – consent of most of the Western governments, and we can continue to enjoy their support only if news of our activities is limited to those who simply *must* know about us. If I loosen my concepts of security, I diminish my capabilities, and that, I will not tolerate. So, with a free hand, Minister, and under no other circumstances, I will stamp out your Xiristas before they turn your whole camp into a bloody battlefield, which they're well on their way to doing. We'll infiltrate them, we'll judge their capabilities, and when the time is ripe, we'll hit them.'

Infiltration . . . it was the crux of the whole matter. And with Heinnemann dead, with Edgars out of action, there was only Miguel Sampaio left. One man . . .

Paul said: 'Sampaio, is he safe?'

Edgars grinned: 'A great guy, that Sampaio. As soon as they found out about Heinne and me, Miguel was one of the first out there with his whip, he was like to kill me, to prove to them what a damn fine Xirista he is. And then, that night, he cut me free. Too late to help Heinne, but . . . he cut me loose, and I got the hell out of there.'

'All right. Are you ready to move on?'

Edgars nodded. His strength, his confidence were coming back, and he thought wryly: Is it the Irish whiskey? Or just having Paul Tobin beside me?

They clambered out of the swamp on to the wet turf, and threaded their way down the dark jungle trails that jaguars had made, and swam the turbulent rivers and climbed the dark mountain, and when they reached the camp at last, Paul Tobin called for Rudi Vicek, head of communications, and said urgently:

'Get me Major Bramble. In Rio.'

CHAPTER TWO

RIO DE JANEIRO.
Co-ordinates: 22.53S   43.13W.

It had been a long time since Major Bramble had been able to relax – at least momentarily – and soak up the sun with nothing to do but think; and maybe worry a little, too.

Huge and bulky, his skin baked red by the hot sun on the Copacabana beach, he sat cross-legged like a shining Buddha and watched the tight little girls in their tight little bikinis as they wandered past him.

There was a gun under the towel at his side, and behind and around him, strategically placed, were three of his best men, lounging lazily and enjoying the cool breeze that came in from the blue water, their pistols hidden under loose beach robes.

There was Manuel, the young Brazilian, glad to be working at last on his home ground; and there was Roberts, who had once been on the Annapurna Expedition, a volunteer porter to the high, Tibetan snows, and was now eyeing the tall phallic emblem that was the Sugar-Loaf Mountain, and wondering if he could climb it without pitons; and there was Confolens, tall and slim and immensely dignified, with immaculate white hair and the figure of an athlete . . .

Nobody – except the Colonel back in London – knew just where Confolens came from. He spoke English, and French and German, and Czech, and Spanish, and Portuguese to perfection; he was known to have crossed the South American continent at its widest point from Recife in the State of Pernambuco, to Guayaquil in Ecuador, alone, on foot and by water, taking three years over the project and coming out at last with the most erudite studies of the Amazonian Indians that had ever been compiled – and with three bullet holes in his neck and two spear scars in his chest. He seemed never to move his head; but behind the dark glasses the eyes were watching, always watching, and there was not a man on the beach who came within fifty feet of Major Bramble who did not get the closest possible scrutiny from

Confolens. He lay stretched out on the hot white sand, an animal in repose, always alert, always ready, and always supremely confident.

Bramble knew the cypher book by heart, and was very proud of the achievement. It had taken him ten days of concentrated study. There were two thousand seven hundred and twenty-eight four digit numbers in it, each one representing a word or phrase or a combination of letters; and once, as an intellectual exercise, he had put the first eight stanzas of the Divine Comedy in cypher, and had sent them off to Betty de Haas in London, marked 'Personal and Top Secret'. It had taken four hours out of her hard-pressed day to decode them, and she had not been amused by it at all.

But now, he could read all of Paul Tobin's dispatches, even the names (which were always laborious to encypher) without once referring to the keys. He tucked the sheet of paper into his waistband, and went over to where Confolens was, and lay down on his belly beside him and said quietly: 'Paul's worried about a woman named Cheleiros, who appears to be a much distrusted member of the Xiristas. A woman . . . is what I'm thinking possible? Hard to believe, but . . . what do you think?'

Confolens was watching the pineapple seller down the beach, a tall, thin *caboclo*, half white, half Indian. He said lazily: 'Did you ever see a pineapple seller who was not Negro? You can't really tell here, can you? But the social distinctions here . . . That's not realy a *caboclo*'s job, not even in racially-tolerant Rio, is it?' He waited as the man went past, his wicker basket on his head, his knife dangling from a thong at his wrist, and then he said: 'And he didn't even offer us a slice of pineapple. But I got his photograph for the album, so I suppose we should be happy.' The little Minox was always with him.

Bramble frowned. 'Watching us? I don't like that.'

'No, I don't think so. You see the two people under the orange umbrella there? The fat man with the lovely woman? I don't know her, but he's Captain da Costa, General Faleira's aide de camp. You find that interesting?'

Bramble said sharply: 'Yes, I do, he's supposed to be in Sao Paulo. And what's he doing wasting his time on the beach?'

'That's exactly what I was wondering. Tell me about Cheleiros.'

'Nothing much to tell except that . . . the three men who infiltrated the Xirista army, one of them's dead, Heinnemann, and one of them, Sampaio, is still operating successfully. The other,

Edgars Jefferson, got hold of a dispatch from Xiri to Santarem and copied it, it's most interesting. It seems that a woman named Cheleiros is marked for execution, because they don't trust her any more . . . '

'So she has been one of *them*.'

'Yes. Paul thinks it might be the lovely Estrella.'

For a long time, Confolens was silent, and Bramble lay back on the sand and waited. He said at last, very carefully:

'It's a question of time, isn't it? Cheleiros, not a very common name, but . . . no, the coincidence is too pat, it doesn't ring true. Estrella Cheleiros has been General Faleria's mistress for – what – about two years? The Xirista movement is just two years old, and if I were Juan Xira, yes, I'd try my damndest to get to the woman who was the mistress of my most deadly enemy. Xira's a persuasive man, we all know that. I think it's a distinct possibility.' He stared for a while at the pineapple-man, and said, frowning: 'Yes, if she's been working with them, it would account, in part, for their knowledge of almost every move the government makes against them, something that has always puzzled us. Do they know that we've got her name?'

'Precisely the point that Paul made. They surely do.'

'Let's assume that Xira's Cheleiros is the Estrella we know. If we watch her carefully, she's going to betray her knowledge that her secret is out in the open. An attitude would be enough, a tightened suspicion, an added wariness . . . but there's an easier way, that might offer very considerable benefits to us anyway.'

'Oh?'

Down the beach, the pineapple-seller had squatted down close by the orange umbrella, and was expertly shucking one of his fruits, spearing the circles on the tip of his knife and offering them to the two people there. The girl was laughing as the juice ran down her throat and on to her breasts, and Confolens murmured: 'Excuse me . . . ' Bramble heard the tiny click of the little camera before it was tucked away again. He said: 'What's the easier way?'

Confolens touched the short-cropped, white moustache.

He said: 'We kidnap her. You know about *paracurarine*?'

Bramble frowned: 'Pharmacognosy's a bit outside my field.'

'Up in the north, in its crude and more potent form, the Indians call it *urirareri*, one of the many forms of curare. It's an anaesthetic; a man gets a poisoned arrow in his gut they rub *urirareri* into the wound while his friends dig it out with the point of a spear. It's also a very powerful hallucinogenic. Properly administered, it will put Estrella Cheleiros into a quiet coherent coma, and she'll wake up with no more than the idea of a bad dream, after she's told us everything we want to know. It's safer than sodium pentathol, and far more reliable.'

Bramble hated it. 'And you know how to administer it properly? Safely?'

Confolens shrugged: 'I know enough.'

'She won't . . . die?'

'A touch of amnesia afterwards, nothing worse than that, I promise you.'

'Needle?'

Confolens smiled: 'No need to make it difficult, Bram. No, I'll find a way to slip some into her food. There's a pharmacist I know who'll prepare some for me in liquid form, it won't be hard.'

Bramble thought it over. He said at last: 'All right. What do you need?'

'Carte blanche.'

'All right, you've got it. God help you if anything happens to her. The Colonel will have your guts for garters, after I've finished with you.'

'Yes, I'm aware of that.' He was stroking the white hair, patting it precisely into place. The constant smile playing at the corners of his lips, he said, 'There's a reception for General Faleira tonight, at the Palacio Magalaes. I can arrange to be invited there . . . '

'And if you can't?'

'Oh, but I can.' He said dryly: 'I'm a much sought-after guest in Brazil, didn't you know that? A social lion.'

'Tonight. That's not very much time for planning.'

'So if you'll dismiss me now, I'll get on with it.'

Bramble sighed; was the fellow mocking him? You could never tell with Confolens. He said: 'All right. Who will you need?'

'I'll need Roberts, Cass Fragonard, and . . . yes, Efrem Collas. That should be enough.'

'It won't be easy to get her out of the Palace.'

'If it were, you wouldn't need me, would you?'

'Well . . . I want the plan by seven o'clock. We'll meet then, in the cellar.'

'It'll be ready by then.' Confolens turned his head and studied the orange umbrella for a moment. The girl had finished eating and was stretched out on the sand, her skin shining; da Costa was leaning back in his deck-chair, his eyes covered with walnut-shells to keep out the bright sun, a touch of white cream on the end of his nose. Confolens said gently: 'Watch out for the pineapple-man.'

'You said he was after da Costa.'

'I could be wrong, of course. I sometimes am. Rarely, but once in a while. He might be on to you, to all of us.'

It was a small victory; Confolens gave it to him willingly; you could always tell when Bramble was worried. *He can't dissemble,* he was thinking, *a good man, but too straight-forward, no deviousness about him . . .* He thought to himself: *And I could be wrong there, too.*

The dark glasses were masking his eyes. He looked at Bramble and said softly: 'Supposing that *caboclo* is after da Costa. Do you want us to do anything about it?'

Bramble said tartly: 'No. We can't risk our cover for the sake of one man, especially a man like da Costa. He's the kind of man who gives the Xiristas whatever popular support they have . . .'

'And that's not much.'

'No, but . . . they point to da Costa and say, that's the enemy, that's the menace we're fighting, join with us. And some of them do. No, if they're after da Costa, we'll just have to let them take him.'

'You're in command.'

'And I will not risk our cover for anything. Anything, or anybody. Especially not da Costa.'

Confolens nodded. He climbed to his feet, tightened the belt on his bright green robe, and went back to the hotel.

The cellar had long been abandoned, when the new restaurant had been built on the summit of the Pao de Asucar, the great Sugar-Loaf mountain, and the old one had been allowed to fall into disuse and disrepair.

It had once been the wine cellar, and its single window overlooked the whole of Rio and Niteroi, the gorgeous beaches, and all the grey-green islands that were scattered, in spectacular disarray, all over the great blue bay. The door was locked, as it had been locked for fifteen years, and the janitor who lived on the other side of it, in a single room that had once been a kitchen, had recently been replaced by his 'cousin', who was a corporal in Colonel Tobin's Private Army.

He was with them now, switching the controls of the sensor that would tell them if anyone were approaching the underground complex, watching the black-and-white dials carefully. As they waited for him to give them the all-clear, he said: 'There

18

were three plainclothes police up here this morning. Off duty.'
He grinned. 'My papers are in order, and they found nothing
in here to interest them.' He switched off the controls. 'All clear,
I'll take it into the other room.'

He left them, then, the six of them, sitting on wooden benches
that were kept free of any tell-tale dust that might betray their
presence; Bramble, and Confolens, and Roberts, and Cass
Fragonard, the Frenchman who walked on two aluminum legs,
and the two representatives of Intelligence Group Seven. There
was Jorge, the young Brazilian from Manaus who had infiltrated
the Police Department; and Nicola da Santis, a bright-eyed
young woman who had recently joined the staff of the *Jornal do
Brasil* and was fast becoming their most expert crime-reporter.

Confolens spread the map out on the plank table, and tapped
it lightly with a well-manicured finger. He said:

'Here, the Great Hall. The stairway that leads to the main
rooms on the upper floor, and then on to the bedroom. Fragonard
will be on the verandah, here, and immediately below him, waiting in the shrubbery just beyond the kitchen door, Roberts and
Efrem Collas will be in the uniform of the National Security
Guard.'

Bramble said peevishly: 'Collas ought to be here now, where is
he?'

Confolens smiled thinly: 'Collas is out checking on da Costa.
General Faleira arrived at his house this evening without him,
and with four bodyguards instead of the usual two, so it occurred
to me that we ought to find out if there's any special reason for
that.'

'And is there?'

'We'll know soon, I hope. All we've run into so far is a blank
wall of obstinate silence. A mystery there somewhere . . . Collas
is trying to unravel it. Unless Nicola has some news for us?'

She shook her head: 'Nothing. I don't feel I can ask too many
questions . . . if he turns up dead, too many people would want
to know why I was so interested.'

Watching her, listening to her careful avoidance of her natural
Lisbon accent, admiring the way she slurred the *l*'s and the *t*'s
in the local fashion, Confolens remembered his first meeting with
her, when Paul had introduced them. He had studied her then,
and had said to Paul, after she had gone on her way: 'How is it
that every single woman the Colonel hires is not only talented,
but . . . astonishingly beautiful?'

He remembered Paul's amusement, the broad deprecatory

shrug: 'The kind of money we pay, there's not a man or a woman who wouldn't come to work for us; we get the very best available. And looks are as important as talent. You'd be surprised how easy it is for an attractive woman to get where you and I can't go . . .'

Bramble said, 'All right, let's forget about da Costa. Go on.'

'Here,' Confolens said, 'in the Great Hall is the only place I can be sure of finding Estrella, towards the end of the evening, when security might be a little more lax.' He sighed. 'It would be nice if I could get her alone for a while, but I'm discounting that possibility altogether. I'm simply going to slip twenty-seven grains of *urirareri* into her drink. For fifteen or twenty minutes, she'll be perfectly all right, and then her mind will begin to wander, and that's when I've got to get her out of there, fast.'

Bramble said sourly: 'Right under the noses of the General and three hundred-odd guests?'

'Yes.'

'You'll never get away with it.'

Confolens said, 'Nicola . . .'

Nicola da Santis leaned forward, the black hair falling across her face; her voice was deep, almost like a man's; Bramble wondered if she were a Lesbian. She said:

'Estrella recently ordered a pair of emerald and gold cuff-links for the General, from Arnold Filhos, and she's expecting delivery of them in a few days. I'm posing as a saleswoman from the jewelers, and I'll tell her that one of the cuff-links has been finished, and that the goldsmith would like her approval before he goes ahead with the other one. I'll tell her that Arnold Filhos' manager is waiting for her in one of the upper rooms.'

'It's a matter of getting her away from the General,' Confolens said. 'A little secret between two women. Estrella herself will want him out of the way for a few moments. All right so far?'

'All right.'

'Nicola will take her upstairs to the room where Fragonard is waiting on the verandah. He will lower her to Roberts, waiting in the shrubbery below . . .'

Bramble said sharply: 'There'll be no harm done to her.'

'None at all. She'll be in a walking coma, quite unaware of what is happening. Roberts is in the uniform of a Security Guard Major, and he'll simply walk with her through the guards to where her car is parked, and drive off with her.'

Bramble said: 'The keys to her car will be in her purse.' Confolens interrupted him and said: 'Collas will have hot-wired it,

20

ready to go. There'll be no fumbling.'

Major Bramble wished he'd kept quiet. But he was worried about the whole thing; there were too many imponderables. He said at last: 'All right, bring her to the safe house. I'll be waiting there for you. What's your contingency plan?'

Confolens said: 'If anything goes wrong, five of us will simply abduct her by force, as she's leaving the reception.'

'*Their* tactics. That's the way the Xiristas operate.'

'And that's the reason for the contingency. They'll be blamed for it.'

'And everyone's going to get shot.'

'No. We'll be faster than the Xiristas ever thought possible. But a contingency is just that, for emergencies. And, take my word for it, there'll be no need to fall back on it.'

'All right then. What about this damn drug?'

Confolens reached into his pocket and brought out a tiny, almost colorless pill, the size of a pea. He passed it over to Bramble, and the Major rolled it between his stubby fingers and examined it. It was soft and resilient to the touch, and Confolens said:

'The casing is made of rice-paper, it dissolves instantly in liquid. Twenty-seven grains of *urirareri*, and I've got six of them. In the course of the evening, she'll get one of them in her drink, and the rest is just a matter of routine.'

'Your invitation to the reception?'

'It's arranged.'

Bramble knew better than to ask how, or by whom. He said instead: 'Then from midnight onwards I'll be at the safe house. How long do we have to hold her?'

Confolens shrugged: 'By morning, she'll be herself again. We'll have to hold her at least until then.'

'And when she comes round?'

Confolens hesitated. 'The contingency first. If necessary, she'll be halfway up Mount Corcovado, in the gardener's house of the old Hotel Botafoga, it's empty now. But that's just in case we've got the wrong Cheleiros. If it turns out that Estrella is really the woman we're after, and the more I think about it the more I'm convinced that she is, then we hang on to her for as long as necessary. If we can convince her that she's been marked down for assassination . . . ' He shrugged. 'She is a highly intelligent woman, it shouldn't be too hard.'

'Her own intelligence might mitigate against us,' Bramble said. 'She may deduce that the whole thing is a put-up job to get her on our side.'

'It's possible.' He didn't seem too unconcerned about it. 'In any case, her car will be found in Ipanema, where Roberts will abandon it, as soon as she's at the safe house.'

Bramble lumbered to his feet. He said: 'I'm flying north in the morning, I want to see Rick Meyers. It'll be nice if we have something solid to pass on to him.'

'One way or the other,' Confolens said, 'either negative or positive, we'll have something.'

They signalled the janitor and waited in silence till he gave them the all-clear, and then, one by one, they left their shelter and became once more a group of tourists wandering through the lovely hibiscus gardens of the Pao de Asucar.

CHAPTER THREE

The Palacio Magalaes, on the southern slopes of the Morro da Babilonia, had been built in the early seventeen hundreds, soon after the discovery of diamond beds in the State of Mina Gerais to the north of Rio, just before that city became the capital. In those days it had been the home of the Marquis Cisplatina, and later, before their expulsion by the Marquis of Pombal, the headquarters of Brazil's Jesuit priests. It was small, as palaces go, and built of richly-carved stone which had been ferried across the bay from Niteroi.

There were some three hundred guests there to celebrate the fiftieth anniversary of General Faleira's service, all crowded together in the Great Hall under the thirty-foot chandelier that had been brought from Venice a hundred and fifty years ago, its myriad lights scintillating on the polished marble floor. There was a brigade of the Special Guard on duty on the grounds, and four squads of Special Police, awkwardly dressed in tuxedos, were circulating within the Palace itself.

A whole brigade? Confolens had seen three armored cars and heavy machine-guns outside the house, and he thought that it augured badly for his operation. He knew that something unpleasant was afoot, and was equally sure that by the end of the evening, he'd find out just what it was. Or was it merely . . . ?

The whole city was under siege. The figures had just come in, from Nicola da Santis through Rick Meyers; eight hundred and forty-two government officials – some of them good men, some not so good – had been murdered by the Xiristas in the past seven months. And in the State of Parana, eight police posts had been attacked in the last three weeks, the occupants all brutally slain and mutilated. The Xiristas were getting bolder . . .

But now, a delicate glass in his hand, his evening dress resplendent with his miniatures (among them, the Croix de Guerre from France, the British Military Cross and the tiny gold leaf of Poland's Order of Merit) Confolens was watching the General.

General Faleira was in splendid form, a grave and courteous man in his early seventies, his narrow chest entirely covered with his medals and his honors, the gold sash of the Legion slung over his right shoulder. He was a small, wiry man who was still spry and alert, moving quickly among the ladies and kissing their hands with a gracious, old-fashioned gallantry.

Watching him, Confolens thought – the most feared man in all Brazil, and look at him . . . He took his turn in the line, and bowed as he held the General's hand, and murmured: 'Felicitations, Excellency . . .'

The General peered at him. The Major-Domo had announced the name, thumping on the floor with his mace: 'Senhor . . . Confolens, was it? I'm sure we've met. Forgive me . . .'

'It has never been my privilege, Excellency. A dear friend of the Condessa Alpercatas.'

'Ah yes, of course. She has often mentioned your name.' It was a lie, on both sides, the little lie that good manners called for.

Close by the General, a tall young woman in the uniform of the Women's Auxilliary Force was standing, waiting to light his cheroots, to pour his drinks. It was hard to recognise her now, the young, slim body hidden by the tailored uniform; the smooth breasts that had jiggled so nicely under the bikini now held firmly, correctly, in place with the brassiere; khaki, Mark Three, Women's Auxilliary Services; the glowing hair confined now under the smart peaked cap – but it was the woman from the beach, the girl who had been laughing there with da Costa.

And where was da Costa now?

Confolens moved on and smiled at her, and said lightly: 'I don't see da Costa here, I was hoping for a chat.'

He was astonished at the way she stared at him, a hard, long look that seemed to say: 'Who are you? What do you want here?' And then she moved her eyes and was whisking a glass of champagne from a passing waiter's tray, holding it there for the General when he should have a moment's respite; it was a dismissal of him. But he pushed her:

'Will he be here later on, do you know?'

She turned her lovely grey eyes on him and said tightly: 'No, Senhor Confolens. He will not be here. Not tonight, not any more. If you will forgive me . . .'

He bowed slightly, and went on his way. He was looking for Estrella Cheleiros, and he could not find her, but he found instead the senior social reporter of the *Jornal do Brasil*, a middle-aged woman with gray hair who dressed like a teenager, and covered her wrinkles with pancake make-up. He said, smiling broadly: 'Well, my dear Elena, it's been a long, long time. How are you?'

The pancake almost cracked with her smile, her surprise. 'Senhor Confolens! How is it no one told me you were back in Brazil? Are you still worrying about the eradication of our poor Indians?'

He kissed her hand. 'No, my dear Elena, civilisation must roll on, inexorably, and that means that the Indians must go, doesn't it? They're in our way, in the way of progress.'

Her eyes were very thoughtful, searching him out: 'You know very well that the government is trying very hard to improve the condition of the Indians, so what is it you are trying, in your devious way, to tell me?'

He said softly, sipping his drink. 'The Xiristas have also been trying very hard to set the Indians *against* the government. I just wondered how well they were succeeding.'

'The government is not rising to the bait, if that's what you mean. But I'm sure you didn't accidentally bump into me to talk about your Indians.'

He laughed, a frank and open laugh; he was very good at it: 'No, I'm more interested in the mysterious absence of the General's Aide de Camp, da Costa. Surely he should be standing there where that not unattractive young captain of the Women's Auxiliary is?'

She would have raised her eyebrows, but the make-up would not allow it. 'You mean you haven't heard?'

He knew already. It was a cold *frisson* running down his spine. But he said: 'I know he's in town. I saw him today, on the beach at Copacabana.'

'Under his shroud?'

There was a little silence. Then: 'I see. What happened?'

The elderly Elena shrugged:: 'A surfeit of young women, most probably. He was never really happy, da Costa, unless he was in someone else's bed. Preferably between satin sheets. Or cat's fur, he had a fetish for cat's fur, did you know that?'

'No. I'm happy to say my knowledge of him did not extend quite so far. We were just casual acquaintances.'

Her eyes were probing: 'I happen to know that you had never met him, Senhor Confolens. I was with him a few days ago, we saw you at that Swiss Restaurant, what's it's name? Chez Mallot? I said to him: "There's our famous explorer, surely you must know him?" And he looked at you and said emphatically: "No. And I don't think I even *want* to know him." You were with a singularly attractive young woman whom da Costa had been

25

chasing, quite unsuccessfully, for more than two years.'

'Ah yes, I wish I could remember her name. And he was alone when he died?'

Elena said drily: 'I don't imagine so. So many . . . *tarts* on the beaches. But when they *found* him . . . yes, he was alone.'

Confolens said, pushing: 'And he died of . . . of what, exactly?'

'Can you guess?' Now she was pushing him, looking for secrets.

'A pineapple knife, perhaps?'

'No, no marks on him at all, but that's very interesting. I trust you'll fill me in? I sometimes feel my column needs spicing with that kind of recondite information.'

'I take it there won't be an autopsy? If they believe he merely died of . . . overwork?'

'There will be if I suggest to the General that it might be wise.'

She was no one to fool with, and he knew it. He smiled at her, acknowledging defeat because it would pay him to do so, and said: 'All right, I will tell you a story. But not now. A little later on . . .'

'How later on?'

He shrugged: 'A few days. So tell me, is there any suspicion of murder?'

'There is now, isn't there?'

'Of course. But I mean, outside of the two of us.'

'You made a promise.'

'I will keep it.'

She looked into his eyes, a shrewd, piercing look. 'All right, I will accept that. No, there is no suspicion, and yes, he was alone.'

'And the young Captain?'

'Captain Maria Consuelo Santiago. The General has had his eye on her for quite a long time.'

'Hasn't she moved into da Costa's place rather quickly?'

'Oh no, not at all. The General has taken her to bed at least a dozen times before, but nothing . . . serious, you understand? When he learned of da Costa's death, he merely gave the necessary orders, and Captain Santiago moved in.' The eyes were on him again, boring. 'Are you suggesting that it's a *crime passionel*? One of those amusing triangles?'

'No. It's much more likely to be political.'

'I see. And we're whispering, aren't we? The climate in Rio today is not right for whispering, especially not at this kind of reception. Shall we move on?'

He said very carefully, knowing that he could not trust her:

'If, in the course of time, I tell you who killed da Costa, and why, will you introduce me to Estrella Cheleiros?'

Oh, those probing eyes! She said: 'Yes. If you tell me why you want to meet her.'

Confolens shrugged: 'Permit me my little weaknesses, dear Elena. I have seen her from a distance. She fascinates me.'

'Are you prepared to fight a duel with Faleira? He'll send five brigades against you.'

He liked the mockery; it augured well. He smiled and said: 'A man always dies for his stupidities, doesn't he?'

'All right. She'll be here soon. I will present you. But . . . ' She waved a finger at him. 'The greatest secrecy imaginable – if the General finds out what you are up to . . . have you ever been in a Military Prison?'

'Many, many times, dear Elena.' He bowed over her hand again, and left her.

As she watched him go, she was thinking: 'How that man wears his clothes!'

And then, Estrella Cheleiros was there. She appeared at the head of the stairs as though this were the only point at which to make an entrance, a slim, black-haired woman of impeccable loveliness, not a flaw on that white skin anywhere, with grave dark eyes under well-arched brows, the hair piled high on her head and held there with a single diamond pin that could, he thought idly, have paid off the national debt. She wore a long white gown, cut very low at the neck, and save for the diamond in her hair, no other jewelry.

Behind her, the dark, angry-looking man was her uncle, Colonel Itaguari, the head of the Security Police, and as they moved slowly down the stairs together, there was not a man in the great hall who was not watching her, and lusting after her, Confolens thought.

She moved slowly, with an easy articulation of the hips that fascinated him, and she had the smallest waist he had ever seen. The Colonel was close behind her as she moved through the crowd. She was smiling shyly, demurely, a courtesan with the face of a Madonna. The General went to her and embraced her, and they drank some champagne together, and Confolens waited; soon Elena was by his side, saying: 'Now, I think now is the time . . . '

She took him over and presented him gravely, and he bowed and kissed her hand and thought he had never seen a lovelier woman in all his life. It worried him – but only a trifle – that her

27

uncle seemed determined to stay by her side. Was that the added anxiety he was looking for? Or was it merely part of the pattern of her life? The Colonel's niece, the General's mistress? She'd be watched every moment, constantly, unceasingly. He shook hands with Colonel Itaguari, and Itaguari said:

'Ah yes, Confolens, they told me you'd come back. I believe you're off to the Amazon again.'

'Yes, indeed, Excellency. Though I'm honored that my movements should interest your department.'

'Routine, my dear fellow, nothing else. They said you were going to the Tapajos River. Is that true?'

'To that general area. There've been consistent rumors of a small tribe of Indians about whom almost nothing is known, except that they have a four-year religious cycle and worship a feathered serpent. They also are said to carry clubs made of teak studded with slivers of volcanic glass.'

The Colonel raised his eyebrows. 'An offshoot of the Aztecs? They're a long way from home.'

'The similarities are too acute to be left unexplored.'

'Interesting. And to a man of your acumen an irrefutable challenge. But I hope you won't be going there for the next few weeks?'

'I'm still in the planning stage, Excellency. And of course, there are the problems of the necessary permits.'

'Wait a while, Confolens. The Xiristas have moved in there, in force. We've sent a brigade after them. A ragtag army of Indians and *mestizos,* but they're giving us a very bad time indeed. Wait a while.'

He inclined his head and moved on, and he was conscious that Estrella was still, covertly, studying him, moving unobtrusively to him. He smiled at her, and she gave him a cool, appraising look, the kind of look beautiful women give to men who have secret thoughts about them. He murmured: 'He's a very handsome man, the General.'

Why was she so wary of him? 'Yes, he is. Though perhaps distinguished-looking would be a better word. We've met before, haven't we?'

He shook his head. 'Unhappily, no. I've seen you, of course, but . . . always from a distance.' He added the lie: 'The Condessa Alpercatas is a friend of mine.'

'Ah yes, of course.'

'She's spoken of you often. It makes me feel I really do know you.'

'Oh? And what does the Condessa have to say about me?'

He said carefully: 'She suggested . . . oh, of course, she said you were the most lovely woman in a land of lovely women, and she was right, but she also said . . . she feels you are moving in circles that somehow alarm you.'

'Alarm me?' She laughed, a soft and appealing sound; he wished he didn't have to hurt her.

He said: 'Your closest relative, your uncle, is head of the Security Police. Your dearest friend is the General. The two men most feared in Brazil.' Now the warm, dark eyes were very wary. 'It must make you . . . what? the target of certain maniacs?'

'And that's all they are, Senhor Confolens. Maniacs. I have nothing to fear from them, nothing at all.' The contempt for *them* in her voice was considerable; was it too much? Was it put on? 'Besides, I am very closely guarded. We all are.'

Was it a warning?

He said, making little of it: 'The guard seems very heavy tonight, more than I would have expected.'

But she would not take the bait. She nodded: 'It's sad, isn't it, that we can't move around without guns behind us all the time. Life would be so good here if only . . . if only people would have a little more tolerance.'

He felt strangely aware that she knew something that she ought not to know, and he wondered what it was. Was there a leak somewhere? For a moment, the thought disturbed him, and then, as if in answer to those thoughts, he saw Nicola da Santis coming into the room, dressed now in a simple black evening gown, carefully not catching his eye and moving to where the bar had been set up. It was hard not to look at his watch; it was an hour at least before she was due. He smiled his easy smile and said:

'May I get you a glass of champagne?'

'Yes, that would be nice. The Bollinger, if you'd be so kind.'

'The Bollinger.'

He moved over to the bar and told the waiter, and he looked at Nicola; there was no one near her, and she was helping herself to some canapes. She said quietly: 'Trouble. Roberts sent me to tell you. At least eight of *them* in the garden, in uniform.' She looked at him now and said brightly: 'Senhor, *faca favor*, have you seen the Senhora Estrella Cheleiros?'

He looked across the room and pointed her out: 'Over there, Senhorita. The lady in white.'

'Ah yes, of course. I have a message for her.'

It was a question: shall I tell her now?

He shook his head imperceptibly, and went back to Estrella with the glass in his hand, and bowed and handed it to her and said: 'The Bollinger, 1959, a perfect champagne.'

'You're very kind. Will you excuse me?' She swept away towards some of the other guests, and he went back to the bar and said to Nicola, very low:

'In fifteen minutes exactly.' He took a cigar from the silver humidor on the table, and said to no one in particular: 'Perhaps I'd better smoke this outside . . . ' He wandered to the door, strolling, taking his time, smiling and bowing as he moved among the guests, and when he was in the garden he found a dark corner and lit the cigar, letting the match flare for a long time, and when it had gone out, Roberts was there.

The Major's uniform sat well on him, and he thought, incongruously: *If I didn't know, I'd be scared of him.* There was a hard, professional-policeman look to his face. He said politely: '*Boa noite, Senhor.*' There was no one around; their voices were sibilant in the darkness.

Confolens said: 'I got your message. Are you sure?'

'Yes, I'm sure. I suspect that fifteen or twenty of the guards are Xiristas. I identified eight of them, and eight couldn't have got in without help from others, a whole commando unit of them, probably. I can give you their names if you want.'

There was a file of them in Bramble's safe, more than three hundred photographs and two hundred and eighty names.

He shook his head, his eyes scanning the garden, searching. 'No, it doesn't matter, it's enough they managed to get in here. It's something I don't much like the looks of, all the same.'

Roberts shrugged. 'We know they're going to kill Estrella Cheleiros . . . '

'And they don't need more than one man with a high-powered rifle for that. But whatever it is, you know the rules. We don't allow ourselves to be detoured. So I'm pushing the operation forward.' He checked his watch. 'In twelve minutes exactly. I've given her the drug already.' He thought for a moment and said: 'I imagine the Xiristas are all together? Not mixing with the others?'

'Yes, they are. On the north side of the house, all of them. Twenty-two guards there, and at a guess, they're all Xira's men.'

'On the north . . . the kitchens. We mustn't discount the possibility that they may be after her too, though I don't think so, it's too big, so if anyone tries to stop you . . . the real Security Police won't, because of your uniform, but *they* might try and stop you. Shoot your way through them if you have to, I'll send Fragonard down to give you a hand.'

'Good. Collas is standing by too. We'll manage.'

'The car's ready?'

'Yes, hot-wire.'

'Bramble won't be at the safe house yet, we'll have to warn him.'

'I've already done that.'

Yes, Roberts would have done that, of course . . . He said: *'Boa noite, Commandante,'* and moved off, and flung away the cigar as he went back into the house.

The timing was crucial now. A quick look at his watch; six more minutes. He saw Nicola eyeing Estrella, saw her eyes go to the ormolu clock on the wall . . . How much had Estrella been drinking? Too much alcohol would speed up the reaction, and he was watching her closely as she chatted amiably with the General.

He wondered about the heavy concentration of the enemy, and wondered if an attempt was being made on Faleira's life. But again, that would require only one man with a rifle, two at the most. Another kidnapping, then? Of Faleira himself?

Confolens didn't like it.

But . . . *No detours,* Bramble would say. *We came here to fight a major battle, and if a sideline skirmish will betray our position, we stay away from it, it's the major battle that counts.*

A major battle . . . a handful of men against a violent and powerful enemy. He was thinking; *that's the way we operate.*

And then, Estrella dropped her glass; it was enough.

He saw the look of amused surprise on her face, a not-very-serious astonishment at her own clumsiness, and he looked to Nicola to give her the signal: *move in now.* But Nicola was well-trained too – she would be, Rick Meyers had hired her! – she was walking quickly to Estrella, a broad, professional smile on her face. He edged nearer, his back to them, and listened.

He heard her say: 'Your pardon, Excellency . . . ' And then: 'My name is Maria Miguela, I'm with Arnold Filhos . . . '

He heard Estrella's laugh, and then the two women were whispering together, and when he turned, he saw that the General, with great good humor, was watching them move away together towards the stairway. He saw Estrella look back and say, laughing: 'A little secret, I won't be long . . . ' She was perfectly steady on her feet; only the eyes were changing, a touch of glassiness to them that you wouldn't have noticed unless you were expecting it to be there. And even if you did, you would have said: too much of that Bollinger '59!

He saw her uncle move as though to follow her, and his temper hardened itself of its own volition; but then the General put out a hand and stopped him, and said cheerfully: 'It's all right, Colonel, she has a little present for me, I'm not supposed to know about it.' He lowered his voice: 'Gold and emerald cuff-links; don't tell her I know.'

Confolens was already walking across the room and up the wide stairway, passing the two women en route and bowing slightly to them, heading for the room where Fragonard, on the balcony, was waiting.

The corridor was almost deserted, but not quite; a single guard was standing at its end, close by the open window, staring out into the garden; he turned at the sound of Confolens' footsteps, and Confolens said pleasantly: '*O quarto de banho . . . por aqui?*'

The guard silently signalled him in the other direction, but the two ladies were there now, and he flung open the door for them, and said to Estrella: 'Senhora, someone was looking for you, in here, I think . . . ' He hoped it was excuse enough for the guard, and slipped in with them. He was thinking: Goddammit, that sentry's not supposed to be there.

Or was the man one of the Xiristas? In the house already? He decided that he was.

He closed the door carefully, and leaned back against it, turning the key quietly, smiling at Estrella as she looked around the room. Nicola was talking quickly, keeping her occupied:

' . . . And Senhor Arnold himself insisted that we show you the excellence of the craftsmanship, some of the most intricate gold-filigree he has ever designed, and the emeralds . . . absolutely flawless, and matched with a precision he describes as remarkable . . . '

Estrella was blinking her eyes now, very rapidly, and she swayed on her feet just a trifle, recovering quickly and saying: 'And then we went down to the beach for a swim, in the dark, and we took off all our clothes, and . . . ' She turned to him then, and said, puzzled: 'In the dark? No, there was a full moon, what am I saying?'

He was still smiling at her: 'You were telling me where Juan Xira is hiding, Estrella.'

'Juan? I don't know, really. We never know where he is.'
'Not even you?'

'No, I just send him information from time to time, my maid . . . I've only met him half a dozen times, I don't really trust him too much, the things he keeps telling me . . . they can't be true, can they? I was going to fire her when I found out, but she persuaded me that . . . that . . . and I felt sorry for her, too, so when she had her baby I helped her keep it hidden away and her parents never found out, they'd have been terribly hurt . . . '

He had slipped a hand inside the loose neck of her dress, under the bare breast, and was feeling the beat of her heart; she paid him no attention at all. It was racing fast, much too fast.

He said gently: 'You're coming with me, Estrella, we're going to climb down out of the window.'

She giggled, a child enjoying a childish caper: 'Oh good, I used to do that once . . . '

He stepped across the room and flung open the french window, and Fragonard was there, waiting, looking strangely dignified in the unaccustomed uniform of the Security Police, his black leather boots shining. The old Frenchman grinned at him and said: 'Two minutes late, they're waiting.'

'Good.' He looked over the wrought iron railing, and saw Roberts there staring at him; an unexpected light from a small window was casting a pale yellow glow over his face.

He went back into the room and said: 'Come with me, Estrella, and you must hurry.'

'All right.' She was quite steady now, doing exactly as she was told without question, and he took her hand and led her on to the balcony, and lifted her up easily – so light, so fragile! – and then lowered her gently to Robert's waiting arms. He said to Fragonard: 'Go with her, you may be needed, the grounds are full of them, some trouble shaping up.'

Fragonard laughed softly: 'We'll handle it.'

'Yes, I'm sure you will.'

Fragonard swung his two tin legs easily over the railing, and dropped down lightly; Cass Fragonard, they called him, which was short for *cassoulet a pieds*, the aluminum-legged cooking-pot of his native Marseilles. He had lost both his legs in Algeria, but could still move faster, and more silently, than any of them.

Confolens stared into the darkness there for a moment, but he could no longer see them, nor even hear the faint rustling of the bushes. And now was the moment for decision. He made up his mind quickly; there was no time to think long about it.

He went back into the room and said to Nicola: 'The hell with Bramble, I'm sure we can get away with it if we play our cards right. But I'm going to have to throw you to them, I'm afraid. Colonel Itaguari has got to be warned.'

She nodded, not alarmed in the least: 'All right, I'll tell one of the guards.'

'No, you just might select the wrong one, one of *them*.'

She did not hesitate: 'The Colonel himself, then.'

'He'll have you arrested, immediately. He'll want to find out just who you are.'

'I won't give him the time to do that.'

'If he does, we'll find you, of course, and get you out.' He could imagine Bramble's concern, Paul's anger. He said: 'If you can get away under your own steam . . .'

'I can.'

'All right, do that. Tell him . . . all you have to tell him is that the grounds are full of Xiristas, no more than that. He'll know everything that implies, and a lot more too.'

And then, suddenly, a single shot sounded on the other side of the house, distant and muted, and the room was thrown at once into darkness. For the briefest of moments, the lights flickered and came on again, at quarter-power, as the emergency generator took over; and then, all the lamps were out again, and the darkness was all around them.

He reached out and felt Nicola beside him, and said softly: 'Well, we're too late, so I'm not going to have to break the rules after all. Whatever they're up to, we'll have to let them get away with it. Seems a shame, but, well, that's the way Bramble would want it to be.'

He had hardly finished speaking, when the sound of a machine-gun came to them out of the garden below, and he groped for Nicola's hand and dragged her away from the windows, and a second machine-gun opened up and they heard someone scream, and he said, very quietly: 'All right, if we don't go now, we'll never make it.'

He stood on the verandah with her for a moment, and looked over to the north where the shooting was, and he heard a grenade go off, and said quickly: 'Over you go.'

She dropped down silently into the shrubbery and he followed her and ran with her to the kitchen gate, and Efrem Collas was there waiting for them, and saying quickly: 'Do we stop and fight or get the hell out of here?'

Confolens shook his head. He said sourly: 'We run, just like it says in the book, won't everybody be pleased with us?'

And it was a matter of principle, too. Rick Meyers, who ran

the Intelligence Groups of the Private Army, had drummed it into them: *You run from trouble, always; a dead agent is a useless agent, it costs us too much to train you, let the others do the fighting, you run . . . at the sound of the first shot you go to ground.*

They ran.

They ran through the dark trees and across the splendid lawn, and found the rope ladder that Collas had hidden in the branches of the huge casuarina tree, and climbed up over the wall, and with the violent sounds of the battle reaching an angry crescendo now, they raced along the dirt road, with Collas in the lead to show them the way . . .

And when they reached the car, they found Bramble there, waiting, half-hidden by the dense hibiscus hedge that flanked the roadside. He came out from under cover as they ran towards the car, and looked at Confolens and said: 'Well, is your cover blown?'

He shook his head. 'Nicola's, yes. Not mine.'

'Good. Let's get over to the safehouse.' He looked at his watch. 'With any luck, Roberts and the girl should be there by now.' He peered at Confolens in the darkness and said, grinning: 'I feel I owe you an apology. When Roberts told me what was happening, I was sure you'd blow the whole thing by warning them. But you didn't or you wouldn't all be here.'

Confolens squeezed Nicola's arm; he felt her respond. He said dryly: 'No, I thought about it for a while. I decided against it.'

'Good. A good operation, I'm very pleased.'

They climbed aboard, and drove quickly down the mountainside and into the town, and over to the house on the Rua Paula Freitas.

In the early hours of the following morning, a demand was delivered to the *Jornal do Brasil*. It was pinned to the chest of one of the night watchmen, an elderly Negro who slept on the pavement in front of the rear door to the offices, by a dagger that had been thrust deep into his heart; Xira always demanded a dramatic gesture to awaken what he thought of as public apathy.

The note said, in part:

. . . and General Faleira will be executed, together with the rest of our hostages, who are now considerable in number, unless the manifest is published immediately, in accordance with our previous demands, and the prisoners we have listed are released immediately and sent to Algeria as we have already, and constantly, demanded.

Close by, a plain cardboard box that had been left there was found to contain two freshly-amputated hands. There was no note in the box, but a ring on the little finger of the left hand, and a subsequent fingerprint test, showed that they were the hands of General Faleira.

CHAPTER FOUR

CACHOEIRA DO CHACORAO.
Co-ordinates: 5.93S: 56.20W.

At night the silence of the jungle erupted into violent discord. The howler monkeys came out and screamed at each other; the tapirs were whinnying like angry horses; the peccaries were grunting loudly and burrowing noisily through the scrub; the night-time parrots were squawking their alarm each time a predator passed, and in this jungle, the predators were innumerable. The only silent creatures moving were the marching men.

There were one hundred and twenty of them, armed with the West's more modern weapons, dressed in the unobtrusive marching grey of Colonel Tobin's Private Army, splashed over with camouflage patches of brown and blue and jungle green. They marched in squads of thirty men, the lead group moving ahead for twenty minutes – which in this inhospitable forest meant no more than a mile – and then sending the runners back with the all-clear for the other three groups to move on. Soon, when the danger would become more acute, and condition Amber would hold, they would start the leapfrogging, each group in turn taking the dangerous vanguard. But now, speed was the only matter, and they were moving fast towards Xirista Camp Number Four.

They crossed over the fiercely-running Tapajos River three miles above the *Cachoeira do Chacorao*, and turned north along the bank till they could hear the roar of the Great Falls coming clearly to them over the brittle cacophony of the animal sounds around them. Three more miles, and an hour and fifteen minutes later, the trees that closely hemmed the river's edge changed species; there were mostly ferns here, but ferns more than eighty feet high, constantly sprayed with the drifting mist of the Falls. The ground was washed clear now, in great blue slabs of granite where lichen was trailing in tentacles of incredible length, some of them more than a mile long, hanging over the edge of the rocks and seeking out even more moisture from the river itself, a thousand feet below them.

Edgars Jefferson, pointing, said: 'There, at the top of the cliff.'

Had he really *run* all this way? He remembered the lithe and easy movement of Leros as here, just by the edge of the Falls, he had first caught up and scared the wits half out of him at a time when he was sure he was safe. It was always the unexpected that threw a man into terror, the sudden let-down from his own imagined security.

He said: 'I don't know about *now*, but *then*, the first guards were about three-quarters of a mile from the top, twelve men, right at the base of a couple of rounded mountains that looked . . . hell, they've got to be called *tetons* something or other, a mountain that shape always gets to be called *teton*.'

Paul Tobin took out his infra-red night-glasses and stared out at the moonlit skyline. He said: 'Not here. Here, they call them *peitos*, it's the *Pietos da Virgem*, the Virgin's Breasts. Yes, I see them. Which side?'

'Right below from this angle, dead center. Twelve men with three heavy machine-guns.'

'A path?'

'Same like this one, a path if you know where to look for it . . . otherwise, an animal track is about all.'

'If they're guarding it, there's a strong possibility it's the only way into the camp on this side. I want to know. Take Gopa with you, report back in ninety minutes.'

Gopa was the Nepalese from Kathmandu, a Gurkha, a night-fighting precision machine who'd spent his lifetime warring against the Chinese who had occupied Tibet and were now seeking to dominate the mountains of his home. He came forward when he heard his name called softly, a slight, dark, wiry man who could have passed for an Amazonian Indian. He was grinning, the white of his teeth stained with betel-nut juices, and he was softy sharpening his *kukri* on a slip of hard leather; whenever Gopa moved around, all you could hear was the soft sound of the polished steel sliding over the surface of the leather, a constant habit; and the blade could cut a falling hair in two.

The two men set off in the darkness, Edgars as black as a piece of jet, Gopa so swarthy that even the moonlight didn't shine on his face.

And when they were gone, Paul blew the silent whistle that would summon the group leaders around him; the ultra-high pitch of it was picked up on the miniature radios that were built into their high-impact helmets. He sent the runners back for Groups Two, Three, and Four as he waited for them, and when they gathered around him, he said quietly:

'We have only one thing to remember. There are six hundred men in the camp, and they're all heavily armed. We attack with two groups only, which means sixty men. The others stay in reserve. Somewhere in the center of the camp, there's a captured brigade of Brazilian army troops, and they are our objective. We don't know where they are precisely, so there can be no random shooting at all, not a single shot to be fired at anything but a specific target. Revolvers only, no machine-guns, no rifles. I don't want any stray bullets plowing their way through the prisoners. The Senior Officer among the prisoners is supposed to be Major Sinal, but it's highly possible that Sinal, as well as all the other officers, will have been murdered, or perhaps killed when they first made contact with the Xiristas. In any event, we just don't know who's in command of them now. If Sinal is still alive, well and good, he's a capable man and he'll lead his troops out as soon as he knows a rescue is under way. But if he's dead, if all the officers are dead, we must expect a certain amount of confusion. I want Mendoza and Romulo to head straight into the prisoners' compound as soon as we locate it, and get the men out.'

Mendoza, the Mexican, leaned forward, and the pale light of the moon shone on his plump, sweating face. He said softly: 'I have the uniform. I am ready, Paul.'

'You're a Colonel in the regular Brazilian army, so if Sinal is still alive, you outrank him. But in that uniform, you'll be a natural target for any of the Xiristas who see you. It's their policy – shoot the officers first, last, and always.'

'I understand. We come out the same way we got in.'

'The same way. Now, the Reserve has to be in position on the north of the camp by 02.00 hours, and I want them not more than half a mile from its limits. Hanson? You're in command of the Reserve.'

Hanson nodded. A big, athletic man, he'd almost lost an arm last year when a mortar fragment had blown a steak out of his shoulder. He was technically a sergeant, but in the Private Army, no one paid much attention to the question of rank; it was how good you were that counted, and Hanson was one of the best.

Paul said, insisting: 'The closer you are to them, the better, so use your own judgement. We'll drive them on to you, but let them go through your ranks, then hit them from behind. You'll be firing to the north, more or less, so it's okay to use heavy weapons. Just remember we're south of you, and that we don't want any casualties, not from your guns.'

'And if they stand and fight?'

'We'll signal if we need help. Two red, one amber on the Verey. Then you come in fast, but only with short-range weapons. Alaric will have the Field Aid Post; we'll select a spot for it as we move in. Anyone gets hurt, one man takes him to Alaric. One man, unless the wound is critical, then two. Just remember the rule.' It was one of their cardinal tenets: one man must never be alone in the field, not in the kind of wars they were fighting.

He went on: 'They've got plenty of Japanese knee-mortars, so we get in close among them, the easiest way to inhibit their use. They've got at least thirty Browning heavy machine guns, fifty calibre, and I want Carlo and ten of his men to worry about them, about nothing else, just get the Brownings.'

Carlo was an old man by the standards of most of them, a Cuban, silent and taciturn. He said laconically: 'My number three squad, okay.' Number three squad was only four men, but it was enough.

'While Carlo's after the Brownings, everyone else to take targets of opportunity. And above all, no one fires, or talks, or makes a sound of any sort, until the white flares go up. Then . . . in we go.' He paused for a moment. 'And let me stress this. These men are fanatics, and they'll still be fighting long after they're dead, so watch out. The local Indians have been thoroughly brainwashed and have reverted to their old tribal savagery, and the *mestizos* . . . well, we all know how dangerous they can be. Violence, savagery is all they've ever known, so don't expect them to pull any punches. Any questions?'

Hanson said: 'If there are any casualties among the regular Brazilian troops, the prisoners? Can we afford to take care of them?'

Paul sighed. 'We have to. They are a pain in the arse, but they're on our side – or at least, we're on theirs, which isn't the same thing – and we get them *all* out, that's the object of the exercise. Once they're out, we re-arm them with rifles, and send them on their way out of our hair, notifying their H.Q. in Gurupa that they've been rescued.'

Hanson said: 'One other thing. They're almost certain to try and take one or two of us prisoners. What's the drill if they succeed?'

Paul said promptly: 'If they do, you talk your head off. But make sure they believe you're holding something back, it's the easiest way to stay alive till we can come back in and get you

40

out. I want a count from each Group immediately the operation's over. No one leaves the area till every man is accounted for. We rendevous a mile and a half back along the track, where Yehud is waiting with the reserve supplies. Anything else?'

There was only silence.

Paul said: 'All right, let's have some chow.'

The four orderlies broke out the bags of almonds and raisins which were their hard rations, and passed them around, and Paul said:

'Anyone wants some Irish whiskey, there's a case in Commissary, four ounces per man for those who want it. More, if there's enough to go round.'

There was no need to remind them of another of the rules. 'Drink all you damn well want,' the Colonel would say, 'but God help the man I find drunk. Or even slowed down.'

They found shelter under the overhanging bushes. A light rain was beginning to fall, a fine, penetrating mist that soon, they knew, would turn into a heavy rainstorm. The bright moon was still there to see, a nebulous, shapeless glow in the sky. Soon it began to fade away as the storm clouds blew in, and when Edgars and Gopa got back, the rain suddenly came down and pounded them into the earth in its fury.

Paul said: 'Nothing like a drop of rain to drive the enemy into carelessness. They'll all be under cover.' A shadow was moving in beside him, silent and stealthy as a fox; it was Radovic, the young Czech. Paul said: 'Rad? Get me a prisoner, will you?'

'Sure. Only one? Better I get you twenty.'

'No, just one. Look for someone in authority. They won't be wearing any badges of rank, but I want someone who appears to be giving orders. Take your time. Concentrate on that and nothing else. Keep one man with you, make your own choice about that, and if anything happens to you . . . one prisoner, it's important.'

'Okay, Paul. Just like the old days . . . '

Radovic had been fighting with Castro, in the early days before he'd become, as he called it, unilluminated. Paul had laughed when he'd first heard the word: 'Don't you mean disillusioned?' And Radovic had said seriously: 'No, Paul unilluminated. The lights went out, they always do when one man tries to force his ways on them that don't necessarily agree . . . '

He said now: 'You don't mind if he gets beat up a little?'

'Just as long as you bring him out.'

'Okay. You got yourself a deal.'

41

The enemy in the camp were indeed under cover.

They had passed the sentries by undiscovered, the twelve men who were waiting at the base of the *Pietos da Virgem*, and one man was left behind there, the Russian, Valnikov, to take care of them when the white flares should signal the start of the battle. He was waiting there now, fifty feet to the north of them, the three grenades he would allow himself ready, sitting in absolute silence and watching them, a stolid, bearded man with short-cropped, iron-grey hair on which the Tartar hat he affected when Paul or Bramble or Rick Meyers weren't around, was an incongruous reminder of his homeland.

The directional sensors were put to use now. Paul was crouched in the lee of a yellow stone boulder, the little black box with its pale blue pin-points of light in his hand, watching the intensity of the bulbs fade as they picked up the receding signals of the others, sensor to every squad as it moved further and further to one side or the other; the tiny blue lights went on and off three times as each squad found its position, a wide arc of deadly, silent soldiers surrounding the southern extremities of Camp Four. Soon, all the blue lights were individually bright, as the squads held their positions and waited.

Paul spoke quietly into his walkie-talkie, his voice so low it was less than a whisper, a zephyr, amplified by the crystal-ceramic cartridge:

'All right, everyone's where they should be, we go in one minute from . . . now.' The tiny blue lights went out, and Paul checked his watch and counted the seconds, his finger on the trigger of the Verey Light. Forty, thirty, twenty, ten . . . he watched the second hand creep round, and pulled the trigger.

The bright magnesium flare went arching up through the trees, the black shadows moving fast at it went on its course, and Mendoza, the Mexican, in his Colonel's uniform now, was racing there ahead of everyone, the others hard on his heels, moving in from the deadly arch, half-running, half-walking, revolvers ready.

Someone shouted and in the bright light of the flares men were running out of the small pup tents – army tents, he noticed – crawling out and leaping to their feet to fire wildly into the night. The men of the Private Army began a steady, careful fire, not wasting a bullet, not firing except at specific targets; when it was over, they knew, Paul Tobin would be demanding an ammunition count and raising hell with anyone who had been too prodigal.

Watching, his rifle across his back and his revolver held lightly in his hand, Paul saw a deserted machine-gun, the heavy rain pounding down on it, saw two men run to it as Carlo got there and kicked it off its mountings; he saw Carlo fire twice, saw both of the men go down. Applewood, one of Carlo's men, an Englishman, bent down and slipped an explosive charge down its barrel, then raced off as the gun blew up. He fired point-blank at a *mestizo* who came at him, firing a Schmeisser machine-pistol as he came, and blew the gun and half the man's stomach away with a single shot.

And now, there was chaos around him. The enemy from the camp were pulling back, in surprising good order, heading north and firing as they ran. A thrown grenade landed at his feet, and he hurled himself to one side, knocking one of his own men – Breton, was it? – off his feet and holding him down till it went off; a fragment embedded itself in his shoulder, a tiny fragment not much bigger than a pea; he felt it crack the bone, and switched his revolver to his left hand.

Group Two was moving forward now, with Group One in support, and though the sound of firing was shattering his ear-drums, there was not one of his own men to be seen. They were all under cover, moving as they had been trained to move, the long line advancing slowly, methodically, inexorably. He saw Tosa Satsum, the Japanese who was leading Group Two, come out from under cover and fire the red-and-yellow Verey Lights that were the signal for Group One to start the leapfrogging, moving past Group Two into the number one position.

The machine-guns were firing still, at least eight of them, and a swath of bullets tore through a barrel of kerosene behind which he was sheltering, and ripped it wide open; the stench of it was insufferable. And then, two of the guns fell silent, and then a third and a fourth, and as he ran forward to take up the line again he saw Carlo's men firing steadily with their Webleys at three of the guns that were being carted to the north. Applewood was in there among them, and he saw him knock two men to the ground with the hilt of his brass-knuckle knife – a relic from his days in the Malayan revolution – and blow up another of the guns with his explosive rods.

And now all the machine guns were silent and there was only the sound of the enemy's rifles interspersed with the sharper crack of their own revolvers. He had measured the distance, and found they had come just over a quarter of a mile from the northern extremity of the map. A few hundred yards more, and they would be running into Hanson's men. He blew three short blasts on his whistle, the signal to retreat, and watched as the line fell back, in good order, seeking cover where it could, still firing at targets of opportunity.

And then, Mendoza was beside him, and Romulo, the Argentinian, was with him too, and they were alone. Mendoza was staring around, he was bleeding badly from a cut across the side of his head and he said savagely: 'No prisoners, Paul, not any more.'

Paul said: 'All right, fall back with the others.'

He blew six short, sharp blasts on his whistle, the signal for silence, and most of the firing stopped; there was just sporadic rifle-fire now, coming from the north of them, the bullets clipping their way through the foliage with an oddly incisive sound. The animals were silent, silenced by the mayhem, by the sounds and the scents of battle, and he could faintly hear the voices to the north as the enemy regrouped. More than half a mile away, he was thinking, right in Hanson's lap. And then, the orderly bursts of machine gun fire started up again, only this time they were Hanson's, and now, he knew, the battle was over.

He fired the purple shell from the Verey that meant rendezvous.

He turned to Mendoza now: 'No prisoners? How sure are you?'

Mendoza's eyes were on fire. 'I am sure, Paul. A mass grave, over there,' he pointed. He was dabbing at the cut on his head, trying to staunch the flow of blood, and he said: 'I found one Xirista, still alive after I killed him, just like you say, not wanting to die. He told me. This morning they kill all the prisoners, one whole brigade, eight hundred men. All the officers, they murder three days ago. Now, today, the order come in to kill the soldiers too, they don't want to bother with prisoners.'

'Came in? From whom?'

Mendoza said 'The order came from Juan Xira, personally.

'All right. Get back to the Field Aid Post, get that wound seen to. Then on to the rendezvous.'

There was silence all around him now, and he had the uncanny feeling that he was quite alone, that none of his men had survived; he could not even see the movement of bushes as they made their way carefully back through the undergrowth. He reloaded his Webley and moved off after them.

The rendezvous was in the shelter of the largest tree he had ever seen. Up in the platforms of its lower forks, four machine gunners were waiting, and at the very top, Rudi Vicek had climbed with the sensor and the infra-red glasses that were all the tools he needed to make sure that none of the enemy was still prowling around; they did not suffer defeat easily, the Xiristas.

They spoke in whispers, the Squad Leaders making the count as men came straggling in. Fourteen had been wounded, eight of them seriously; only three had to be carried back to base.

And Radovic was there waiting for him, with two bullet-holes in his body, one in the upper arm and one through the neck, with the medics swabbing out the wounds with iodine as he grimaced at the pain of it.

Grinning, he jerked a grimy thumb at the recumbent form at his feet, a small, thin man of about forty years or so, dressed in nondescript khaki slacks and bush jacket, a bandage over his eyes and his wrists tightly lashed with a leather thong; there was a thin rope around his neck, the other end fastened still to Radovic's waist. He said: 'A captain, at least, he was giving his orders with one hell of a lot of authority.' He winced as the medic began swabbing the wound at his neck, saying cheerfully:

'In one side and out the other, a three-eight, too, you ought to be good and dead. Another half millimeter one side or the other . . . '

Paul crouched down on his heels beside the prisoner and took the bandage off his eyes – dark, dark, eyes deep-set under heavy brows; and they were frightened. The cross on the thin chain round his neck was solid gold, and quite heavy, and he looked at the prisoner's hands and found them reasonably well-manicured, not the ill-kept hands of a jungle-fighter at all.

He said pleasantly: 'I can put you under with drugs, I can fill you so full of Irish whiskey you won't care whether you're talking or not, I can carve you up with a bush-knife. But, one way or the other, I can get from you the information I need. So which is it to be?'

The man did not answer, and he said: 'Or I can simply hand you over to the Brazilian authorities and let them find out for me the things I want to know. If I do that, you'll be charged with armed insurrection, and you'll undoubtedly be executed.' He said, musing: 'It never seems to occur to you people that your kind of terrorism invites retaliation in kind, does it? You push the atrocities harder and harder and you still expect them to fight you with gloves on, it doesn't make sense.'

There was a little silence. Then: 'I claim the rights of a prisoner of war.'

Paul said: 'A prisoner, yes. But this is not really a war, is it? And believe me, I have no concern at this moment for the Geneva Convention. What happened to all those soldiers that were murdered?'

It was by no means question number one; but he was gratified at the excess of terror in the man's eyes. He said quickly: 'I had nothing to do with that. I argued against it. I am an officer, not a murderer.'

They were talking Portuguese, and Paul switched to Spanish and said: 'But not a *Brazilian* officer. I think you're more at home in Spanish, aren't you? Suppose you tell me who you are? You are not a Brazilian.'

Another silence, a long one, and then: 'In exchange for what?'

It was the easiest way. Paul said, shrugging: 'All right, we have no profit in your death. Tell me what I want to know, and I'll see you're released, unharmed. If you don't, we'll kill you, it's as simple as that.'

'All right.' The prisoner hesitated, and Paul said gently: 'You have my word. First, tell me who you are.'

He was still not sure. 'And you'll release me?'

'In a day or two, you have my word.'

'All right.' A shudder ran through his body; was he making up his mind to tell the truth? Or wondering how far he could distort it? He said at last: 'I am Major Roberto Pereira San Borja de Quemada.'

'Of what army?'

'Of the . . . of the Bolivian Army.'

'I see.' Paul thought about it for a while. Overt support for the Xiristas from the Bolivian Government? He thought not. He said: 'A renegade, I suppose?'

'No. We don't call ourselves renegades.'

'No?'

'We are volunteers, helping the Xiristas, we're on leave from the Bolivian Army.' It didn't sound right.

He got up abruptly and said: 'All right, I can only keep my bargain if you tell me the truth.'

As he began to move away, the Major said hastily: 'Wait.' He turned back. The Major said: 'You know about General Ramon Huachi?'

'Ah yes . . . ' Paul squatted down again beside his prisoner, and said: 'This gets very interesting. Huachi heads an extreme

46

right-wing group that's been outlawed by your army, a price on their heads. And yet you're helping Juan Xira, who is an avowed Maoist. The reason ought to be quite intrigueing.'

'If Juan Xira gets his way, he'll rule Brazil.'

'And then?'

The Major laughed shortly, a small, sardonic laugh, still tinged with the fear: 'An incompetent government such as Xira would head . . . we can get back the border provinces they stole from us, the diamond mines in Guapore, the gold in the Planalto do Mato Grosso . . . We can present them to Bolivia and regain the authority that was stripped from us.'

'You've got a nice middle-of-the-road government now, why don't you leave it like that?'

'Bolivia must take her rightful place again in the scheme of South American affairs. We need a strong government, an authoritarian government . . .'

'Oh God, here we go again. An *authoritarian* government? I take it you don't have the authority of the people in mind?'

'The people have been brainwashed by the Communists.'

'And your brainwashing is better?'

'Ours is the authority of discipline.'

Paul said, knowing it was no good: 'And so you turn the Maoists to your own ends.'

The Major shrugged, the fear receding now: 'They, too, use everyone who might help their cause. We merely took a leaf out of their book.'

'Who ordered the mass murder of those soldiers?'

'Juan Xira. He had the officers killed as soon as they were captured, and his lieutenants wanted to hold the men as hostages. Xira said they wouldn't be needed as hostages, that they'd be too much of a burden.' He paused. 'This is the way the enemy works. Ruthlessly.'

'The enemy you support. They're using rifles from Ixiamos.'

The Major hesitated; he had already talked too much. But he said: 'Ixiamos is where General Huachi is hiding. He's well equipped.'

'A revolution of your own?'

'One day, perhaps.'

'And meanwhile, the whole of Brazil is in flames. Eight hundred political murders in the last seven months, in Rio, Sao Paulo, and Belem alone. Two thousand casualties in the Brazilian army, and God knows how many of your brainwashed Indians have been killed.'

47

'We do not call it brainwashing. We say rehabilitation.'

'It's hard to rehabilitate a dead man's family.'

The Major shrugged. He was confident now, carrying the ball himself: 'If an older generation must die so that a new one can live in freedom, that is the way it has to be.'

'Your kind of freedom? Or Juan Xira's? They're both false, aren't they? You're spouting the philosophy of the fanatic.'

The Major was watching him, the dark eyes probing. He said: 'Tell me who you are. Tell me which side you are on.'

'Who we are? No. What side we're on? I suppose you could say we're on the side of the Revolution. But the last one, not yours.' He tried hard not to sound sardonic; there were always the revolutions here, a constant factor, and only stability could put an end to them. He said: 'And tell me where the main force of your Xiristas is hiding out.'

'You promised me my freedom.' He was holding out his bound wrists, and Paul took his knife and sliced through the ropes. The Major lifted the nose off his neck, a symbolic gesture; and then he began to lie.

He said carefully: 'Their main force is concentrated around Manaus and Belem.'

'How many of them?'

He shrugged: 'Forty, fifty thousand, perhaps.'

'And in Rio itself?'

'No more than a few hundred.'

'The heads of their groups?'

'I do not know who they are.'

'But you know who runs the group you were attached to.'

Another lie: 'He calls himself Salvador. I do not know his real name.'

'All right, let's leave it at that, at least for the moment. You'll come with us for the rest of the night, and in the morning, after we've had another talk, you will be released.' He turned away and said to Radovic: 'Your prisoner. Watch him.'

The Czech's neck and arm were heavily bandaged now, his rifle cradled across his knees. He nodded, and looked at the Bolivian major and said: 'And while you are among us, friend, don't think you can get hold of a gun. Don't try it.'

The Major said nothing, and went over and sat down under the big tree, staring darkly into the night. His eyes were veiled, and in a little while he closed them, made himself more comfortable, and went to sleep.

The men were all in now, the last stragglers snaking their way back from Camp Four, Hanson bringing up the rear-guard with eight men strung out on each of his flanks. Rudi Vicek set up the short-wave UHF radio, and Paul spoke to Bramble in Rio.

Bramble said cheerfully: 'I won't stay on the air, Paul, we're meeting tomorrow. At point ninety-two, can you make it?'

'Point ninety-two?' He was flipping the map open, shining the pen-light on to it. In the wet air, the heavy rain still drumming down, the reception from the micro-miniaturised set was remarkable. Still on the classified list, the radio was no bigger than three packs of cigarettes, but its effective range was eight thousand miles for transmission, twelve thousand for reception. Its mercury-platinum energiser was the size of a matchstick.

'Ninety-two? Yes, I'll use the helicopter. What's happening?'

'A message from the old man in London. He's bringing a guest there.'

'Ah, good. Time?'

'As soon as you can make it. He's there now, and I'm flying up first thing in the morning.'

'The guest is who I think it is?'

'Probably. I have no definite news on that myself. What about the operation?'

Paul said: 'Successful. Only the patient is dead.'

'Oh my God.' He could hear the deep concern in Bramble's voice: 'The Colonel's not going to like that at all.'

Paul said dryly: 'It doesn't exactly please me either, Bram. I'll see you at ninety-two tomorrow. Over and out.'

Ninety-two was the tiny village of Caxiuna, on the eastern bank of the Xingu river, where it broadened out into the great stormy lake some fifty miles from Garupa at the wide and swampy mouth of the Amazon itself.

He said to Vicek: 'The helicopter, where is it now?'

Vicek was head of Communications. He turned the roll-map on his radio, lit it with the pen-light, and said: 'Here, standing by in a clearing at Cupari, it can be here in forty-five minutes.'

'All right, bring it in. Where's the nearest safe landing?'

Vicek said promptly: 'A mile and a half due east of here, a patch of burned-out pampas grass. You want the co-ordinates?'

'Too close, I don't want to attract any attention.'

The map was rolling slowly, and Vicek was peering at it: 'Three miles further on, open country where the Tapajos River meets the Crepori.'

'Good, give the co-ordinates to the pilot, tell him to come in on the finder, oh, two hours from now, not to land till I signal him, okay?'

He called Hanson over, told him to take the Army back southeast to its base, and set off alone along the damp jungle trail that would take him to the confluence of the Tapajos and the Crepori. He moved like an animal in the night, quickly but in silence, his soft shoes running lightly where the ground permitted it, and cutting his way through with the machete when the vines and *llianos* closed tight around him.

And at four thirteen in the morning, he signalled the helicopter in and flew to Caxiuna.

CHAPTER FIVE

CAXIUNA.
Co-ordinates: 02.48S: 52.45W.

Colonel Matthew Tobin was out of his cot as soon as the first rays of the equatorial sun struck across the wide river-mouth and cast its striated shadows over the bamboo walls.

He stood on the verandah, listening to the early-morning sounds that were coming to him from the village further down the bank, watching the Indian children as they splashed in the shallow water. A towel round his taut waist, he clenched and unclenched his hands as they gripped the railings, feeling the strain of the tightening muscles all the way up to his shoulders. He called out softly:

'Charles?'

'Sir?'

She was close behind him, standing in the doorway that led to the bedroom, very tall, almost as tall as he was, slim and svelte and elegant, her hair not yet done and falling down over her shoulders, a cascade of ash-blonde-yellow-saffron.

He turned to look at her, to admire the cool freshness of her; long, slim khaki trousers and suede ankle-boots, with a patch-pocket bush-jacket that was opened three buttons down, the V between her breasts open down to the tight suede belt; the long hair dangling there gave her an oddly intimate look. She carried the little silver coffee-pot on a bamboo tray, the single Stafford-shire cup beside it. He gestured at the rickety table: 'There, Charles. Bring your own cup, we have to talk.'

'All right.'

Pamela Charles, age thirty-three, height five feet ten, weight one hundred and twenty pounds (constantly); she was his aide de camp, his personal servant, his confidante, his memory bank, and his intellectual exerciser. She had been with him now for – what was it? – three and a half years? He wondered how he'd ever managed without her.

She had put down the tray, and now she came with her own

51

cup and pulled out his chair for him, facing the river, and sat down beside him and poured the coffee, and placed one small lump of sugar in it and carefully stirred it, and then sat back and waited for him to begin.

He watched the naked children in the water for a moment, stared out at the long row of mangrove trees that lined the river's edge. A small outrigger canoe was putting out, three men aboard with nets and small spears; further along, a decrepit launch was tied up at a tumble-down wharf of adze-cut timbers, its white paint peeling, its smoke-stack blackened, a huge pile of lumber ready for loading close beside it; it was already lurching drunkenly in the muddy water.

He saw that her notebook was on the table in front of her, her pencil ready. He sipped his coffee and said: 'All right, first things first. What time is the Minister getting out of bed?'

She was smiling faintly: 'He left instructions with his orderly not to wake him before ten o'clock.'

'Get him out of bed at seven.'

'All right.'

'Paul should be here soon after that, and Bramble by about nine. What about Rick Meyers? Where is he? How come he's been off the air all day yesterday?'

'He's still in Rio. Major Bramble is bringing him too.'

'Good. Set up the meeting for ten, I want to see Paul, Bramble and Rick as soon as they come in. Tell the Minister I want this place surrounded with his troops. Tell him mine are too damn busy doing his work, he's got to look after the security as long as we're here. But check on it yourself. Where's Betty de Haas?'

'She is swimming.'

'Ah, good. What about the new maps?'

'She collated them very early this morning, they're back on board the plane, in the safe.'

'Plane's under guard?'

'Yes, of course.'

'Tell the Minister, too, that I will want an up-to-date pin-pointing of . . . let me see . . . ' He leaned back in his chair and put his feet up on the railing. A *gekko* on the ceiling was watching him, absolutely motionless; it changed its color from grey to blue as he watched it, and the swivel-eyes found a spider making its web in the near corner; it did not move. The *gekko*, too, was waiting, he thought, waiting for the right time to strike.

He said: 'The Fourth and Eighth Battalions ought to be in

the swamps around Maues somewhere, but they're probably not. In any case, I want to know exactly where they are and I want them out of my hair . . .'

'Withdrawn entirely?'

'Yes, back to base, where they can't do any damage. And when Paul gets those prisoners out, I want them withdrawn too. There are three Brigades of Artillery, the First, Ninth and Tenth, along the banks of the Tapajos, on the eastern side, and I want them all to cross over and disperse in three different directions. I don't care where the hell they go, but I want the Xiristas to know they're pulling out, and I want them scattered, they're much too strong together to tempt Xira out of his hideout. Tell the Minister I want that put into motion right away, and I want confirmation when it's done.'

'All right. What about Rio?'

'We'll leave Rio alone till I've talked with Bramble. Or, more specifically, with Rick Meyers. What else is there?'

She was lifting the lapels of the khaki jacket away from her shoulder, letting the air over her breasts; six-ten in the morning, and the damp heat was already oppressive, even up here, where there was at least a wind sweeping over the pampas.

She said: 'Paul will want to know about the new aircraft.'

'Ah yes.' He was amused by the way she seemed to curl herself up, even on a canvas chair, her long legs tucked under her. He said: 'I don't suppose he'll find any use for them. They can take off on a tennis court, but there are precious few tennis courts in the middle of the Amazon jungle. Well, we'll see. Accommodation?'

'I thought Paul might like to share your room. I'm putting Major Bramble and Captain Meyers together in the hut by the nut sheds there, it's very comfortable.'

'He'll be hungry when he gets in, I don't suppose he's had much to eat the last few days.'

'I've laid on breakfast, bacon and eggs all round. We brought bacon with us.'

'Ah, splendid, I'll have some myself too.' He looked at his watch. 'Now I'm going for a swim.' He was peering out at the river. 'I don't see Betty down there.'

She pointed: 'The inlet there, deep water, it's much clearer. Just beyond the orchids, there's a small waterfall. I'll get you some towels.'

'Yes, do that.'

She found him a couple of bath towels, and he walked over to where the purple orchids, interspersed with the bright blood-red of climbing hibiscus, were brilliant patches against the living yellow-green of the trees.

Betty de Haas was swimming lazily back and forth across the small pool under the waterfall, quite naked, the water gleaming on her plump little body, her tawny hair cut short and clinging to her head like a boy's. She turned over on her back and kicked out her legs, swinging her arms back and over her head and circling around him as he slipped out of his shorts and dived in. He swam fast, a quick six-stroke, four times across the pool, and then went down deep where the water was icy cold, and swam under water for a minute, counting the strokes before he came up again. He swam to the bank and climbed out, and turned to watch her for a while, and then she joined him and he held out the yellow robe for her, patted her behind, and said:

'They'll all be here in a couple of hours, let's go and have some breakfast.'

The Minister was late for the meeting, and Charles had to go and get him. She had brought him breakfast of coffee and hot rolls at seven (his own orderly was still asleep and could not be found), and he had promptly tried to seduce her, then had gone grumpily back to sleep when he discovered that this was not the purpose for which she had come to his room at such an ungodly hour of the morning. He'd tried once more on the second call, again on the third, and had finally given up when, at seven forty-five, she had carefully upset the now-cold coffee all over his pillow.

He could see now that the Colonel was in an extremely dangerous mood. His own Prime Minister had told him: 'All right, Minister, you outrank him, he's just a Colonel, but you are to put yourself completely under his orders, is that clear? If the protocol worries you, then I'll have to make Colonel Tobin a local, acting, unpaid Field Marshal, and there won't be any problems. No, not *unpaid* . . . ' The sum of money was huge. The Prime Minister had said: 'You do exactly what he tells you to do, or you'll answer to me personally.'

The Colonel, smiling gently, his voice very soft, said: 'I take it, Excellency, that the troop movements my aide spoke of have already been put into effect?'

The Minister sighed. He'd set his heart on trapping Juan Xira himself; it could have meant the Prime Ministry at the next election, *if there's ever going to be one,* he thought.

He said: 'Yes, Colonel Tobin, the messages went out at the crack of dawn this morning.' His eyes were on the plump little dark woman, what was her outlandish name? De Haas? Dutch, then, and probably frigid, but perhaps not, not with that overly-prim look in her eyes, put on, no doubt, for his benefit. He'd seen them both, Tobin and the girl, romping together naked down there in the water, the first time that long-legged blonde creature had tried to get him out of his comfortable bed, and he'd been wondering about it ever since . . .

He said: 'One of the great difficulties inherent in the movements you suggested, Colonel, was the lack of any adequate reason which I can give my commanders in the field. The movement, to them, will look alarmingly like a withdrawal in the face of the enemy. A question of . . . dignity.'

'Yes, of course, I understand. But I leave such matters of military delicacy entirely to your discretion. The essence of the matter is that you have by far too many troops facing Xira, more than sixty-seven thousand infantry alone, and it's quite ridiculous. Xira's men, at our own last count, numbered thirty-two thousand, and although they're well-armed and aggressive, they are not going to attack you while you are so strong. They have no fear at all of your infantry in the field, but they're undoubtedly worried about the heavy artillery, because they don't have any. At least, not very much. And I want him out of his jungle hide-away where I can get at him. And I'm afraid I have some very bad news for you.'

He picked up the report Paul had prepared for him, typed out on six sheets of paper during the helicopter ride, and frowned at it. He waved it at the Minister and said: 'Major Tobin, as you know, decided to combine a probe into one of Xira's camps with an attempt to rescue a brigade of your troops who had been surrounded and captured. It appears they were trapped in the Xeringu swamp, and their commanding officer negotiated terms of surrender with the leader of the Xiristas, a man named Santarem. Under those terms, the whole brigade was to be held hostage for the release of a hundred and seventeen terrorists now in your jails. The terrorists were to be released and flown to Algeria whence, no doubt, they would have immediately and clandestinely returned.' He said sourly: 'Your government's past record in dealing with the eighty-four cases of kidnapping that have been laid to the Xiristas, their prompt accession to the kidnappers' demands, must surely have affected your commanding officer's judgement, so I suppose he cannot be blamed too much.'

The Minister said hotly: 'I'll see that he's court-martialled immediately . . . '

Colonel Tobin interrupted him: 'No, Minister, you will not. The officer concerned was promptly murdered, as were the other twenty-three officers of his brigade. The men themselves were held in Xirista Camp Four, which is where Major Tobin went to find them. I'm afraid that the morning of the day he got there, all the men were massacred. They were cut down with machine-guns supplied by the right wing Bolivian exiles who have been, it seems, actively helping Juan Xira for reasons of their own.' The Minister was staring at him, and he said, choosing to misunder-stand: 'They believe that Xira will win. They believe the govern-ment he installs will be weaker than the present government. They wish to take advantage of that weakness in regard to the disputed border territories.'

The Minister felt that his face was white. He looked at the Colonel's son, Major Paul Tobin, sitting there silently while his father was talking; at the big man they called Bram, who had come up from Rio where he and the Jewish fellow, Rick Meyers, were infiltrating the Xiristas with their own intelligence groups; he looked at the two women, waiting, no doubt, for some sort of response from him. The massacred brigade had been sent out in direct contravention of Colonel Tobin's orders . . .

He said: 'All of them? Murdered?'

'A mass grave.'

The Colonel leafed through the pages again and said: 'Major Tobin's report contains an extract of a statement made by a certain Major Borja da Quemada, a Bolivian exile of General Huachi's group, who have been supplying the Xiristas with their weapons and training them.' He said angrily: 'I warned your Defense Minister in London, when he came to me and asked for my help, that something of this nature was bound to happen, that the Xiristas should be stamped out before every goddam revolutionary group in South America, to further their own ends, came to their assistance. He chose instead to vaccillate, and now . . . now we're fighting an organised and formidable army instead of a fanatical bunch of hot-head terrorists.'

The Minister wondered if the Colonel knew that he himself had sent that Brigade against Camp Four, an attempt to reassert his own authority, a trump card to present triumphantly to the Prime Minister? He thought perhaps not. He said slowly: 'You can count on the whole of the army, Colonel Tobin, for whatever support you need. Once news of this massacre is published . . . '

Colonel Tobin said sharply: 'No, I want your army out of my way. When I agreed to your Defense Minister's request, I stipulated two things. First, that no one, no one outside the three concerned Ministries, would even know of our activities here. Second, that all your military units would be withdrawn from the field and returned to their base before we started work. We've been here two weeks now, and what do I find? You have sixty-seven thousand infantry still fart-arsing around in the Amazon Basin, supported by tanks, heavy artillery, and three squadrons of your Air Force. I find that you yourself sent a full brigade to attack Camp Four which, at that time, contained a minimum of twelve thousand jungle-trained fighting Indians, all heavily armed and well disciplined. You are not only sacrificing your own men, Minister, you are getting in my damn way. And if those troops are not moving back to their bases within twenty-four hours, we all ship out of here, and a report of my reasons for withdrawal goes straight to the Prime Minister.' He stared at the Minister and said coldly 'Now, do I have your full cooperation? Or do I not?'

He was glad there were no other Brazilians there, especially glad that none of his own officers were present. He looked down at the medals covering his massive chest and ran a hand over them, straightening them out; he noticed that Colonel Tobin wore none of his own decorations at all, not even any badges of rank. He nodded, wondering how far he could restrain his apology. He said carefully, protesting: 'I'm afraid I was overzealous, Colonel. It occurred to me that you would need our help, and so . . . ' he shrugged, 'I merely endeavoured to place adequate reinforcements for you in adequate positions. I could not believe, I still cannot believe, that with a force of only . . . how many men do you have, Colonel?'

The Colonel said briefly: 'That's classified, I'm afraid. Forgive me, but . . . ' He smiled broadly, an affable, over-friendly smile that merely made him look more deadly. 'I operate under the tightest security, even at the highest and most trustworthy levels. But I don't subscribe to the theory of blanket-bombing, Minister, if you understand all that blanket-bombing entails. It seems to be a modern military theory that you hit the enemy with too much of everything, that you destroy him by destroying everything that lives and breathes where you think – or hope –

57

that he might be. Well, as far as I'm concerned, that's a lot of balls, and I won't go along with it. The way I operate . . . we search out the head, and we cut it off, skillfully, delicately, and decisively. Do that, and the limbs wither away. We destroy only carefully selected targets, and that's *all* we destroy. In all the years I've been operating, not one man has been cut down who was not palpably, clearly, indisputably an enemy. And that is the way I will continue to operate. Now, to the question of Rio de Janeiro.'

He looked around the table at the others. Major Bramble, red-faced, sweating, perching his huge bulk uncomfortably on his canvas chair; Paul Tobin, sitting back easily with a slight smile on his handsome, suntanned face; Betty de Haas with her folder of maps and notes, her khaki field-dress looking oddly out of place; and Pamela Charles, sitting just the right amount behind him and on his right, impossibly silent and immobile, her long legs crossed, her slim shoulders hunched forward, her glorious hair piled now on the top of her head as though she had just come from London's most expensive coiffeur; and lastly . . . Rick Meyers.

Rick Meyers, the Colonel would tell himself (even half believing it) was the brain of the organisation. Nominally, he was Head of Intelligence and Planning, and he was the one man the Colonel had come to realise he really couldn't do without. A small, dark, wiry man, with shrewd, alert eyes and a sharp and pointed nose, a quiet, methodical man who seemed to get done all the work that was required of him, and a great deal more too, with just no fuss at all. He always knew what you were thinking, and if you were thinking that something was wrong, Rick Meyers put it right before you got around to mentioning it; it was sometimes a disquieting characteristic. And his fertile, imaginative brain was a store-room of all kinds of recondite information.

The Colonel glanced at his watch and realised that in forty-five minutes, no one but the Minister and himself had said a word.

Well, he thought, that's the way it should be . . .

He said now, to Bramble: 'Tell us about Rio, Major.'

Major Bramble cleared his throat and shuffled through his notes. He looked at them briefly, tossed them back on the table, and said: 'First of all, I suppose, the case of General Faleira.' He looked at the Minister and said: 'Do you know, Excellency, that General Faleira has been kidnapped? There's hardly been time for the news to reach you, unless Colonel Tobin mentioned it.'

He saw by the look of shock on the Minister's face that the news was news indeed, and Colonel Tobin said, frowning: 'No, I've said nothing, I don't have all the facts. That has to come from you.'

'Well, in that case . . . Some of us attended a reception celebrating General Faleira's fifty years in the army. A group of Xiristas attended it, too. They have penetrated the Security Police to the extent that at least twenty of them were able to insinuate themselves, in police uniforms, among the guards who were detailed for the occasion, and we're looking into that now. Rick?'

Rick Meyers said quietly, almost nonchalantly: 'Nothing much to report on that score yet, but three of my men have penetrated the Xiristas very successfully, and one of them is already on Xira's Tactical Committee, so I should have some news any day now. Till then, if you don't mind, I'd rather leave it at that.'

'All right,' Bramble went on. 'We became aware of the threat to General Faleira some thirty minutes before the culmination of our own operation, which entailed the abduction of one of the guests. We couldn't interfere without giving our own plan away, so we have to accept it as a defeat. We left three of our men in the grounds to keep an eye on what happened. There was a gun fight between three five-man groups of Xiristas on the one hand, and the real Security Police on the other. I'm afraid that your men were hampered by the fact that the enemy wore the same uniforms. The attack was skillfully planned, and carried out with a certain amount of daring, if not arrogance. Faleira has been removed, and a further demand has been submitted by the terrorists to the government, the usual pattern.' He said gently: 'Only I'm afraid that this time . . . ' He took a long, deep breath, and Rick Meyers said sourly:

'The General's chances of survival seem remote. They have already . . . mutilated him, a lesson to show they mean business. Both his hands.'

'And their business,' the Colonel said, 'is beginning to boil now. Go on, Bram.'

Bramble shifted round in his chair awkwardly. He wished he could get up and pace around, but he cleared his throat again and said: 'Well, they've got Faleira and a lot of other hostages, but we've got one of *them* too, someone who's going to be a great help to us.' He looked at the Colonel, seeking advice, and the Colonel said tartly:

'No need for secrecy, the Xiristas know that they didn't snatch her.'

Major Bramble nodded. He said, enjoying it: 'Estrella Cheleiros.'

The Minister's mouth dropped open. 'Senhora Cheleiros? You mean . . . the General's . . . ? My God, I can't believe it! You *must* be wrong!'

Rick Meyers stood up and went to the table where Charles had laid out the bottle of Irish whiskey and the ice and the glasses. He said: 'It's true, there's no room for any sort of doubt. More important, we've been able to show her documentary proof that Juan Xira wanted her executed. It came as a bit of a shock, and now that the shock has worn off . . . she's on our side now. It's a great help; she's blowing the whole thing wide open for us. As of this moment, we know where most of Xira's men are.'

The Minister said, his voice squeaking: 'You know . . . then you move in and take them, what are you waiting for?' Rick Meyers did not answer him, but just sat there slowly shaking his head, and the Minister turned to the Colonel and said angrily: 'Your own words, Colonel Tobin, you strike at the head . . . '

Meyers said: 'The head is Xira himself. We can pick up three, four, five of his lieutenants tomorrow, but he's got too many good men to choose the replacements from. We want all of them, at once, including Xira himself. That's the way it has to be. Anyone care for a drink?'

The Minister was wiping at the sweat on his neck. He wished he hadn't worn his dress uniform for this meeting; after all, it hadn't impressed anyone, least of all Colonel Tobin, or that lovely blonde animal who sat so still and silent beside him, she'd hardly noticed him at all. He turned and said wistfully: 'Would you have any *pinga*? The local brandy, you know . . . '

Colonel Tobin said cheerfully: 'Irish whiskey, my trademark. You find a bottle of Irish lying around in the jungle, you'll know I'm not far off and can take comfort in the fact. Pour, Rick, and come and sit down.'

Meyers came back to his seat. Unobtrusively, Pamela Charles was there, passing round the tray with the drinks on it, and the Minister said, astonished: 'Ice? Where the devil did you find ice in this god-forsaken hole?'

It was Charles who answered him, and his heart went out to her for her smile: 'There's an ice factory at Para, didn't you know? We sent a boat down the river last night.'

He patted her smooth haunch as he took his drink, and she

60

moved silkily away and took her seat again. But his heart wasn't in it; he was still suffering from his astonishment.

He said again: 'Estrella Cheleiros . . . it can't be true!'

The Colonel said patiently: 'So you said, quite incorrectly, before. And her recent adherence to the Xirista cause opens up a rather interesting subject for speculation. Take over, Rick, the Minister's the only man who can answer your question.'

Rick Meyers said: 'Colonel Itaguari, Estrella's uncle, the head of the Security Police. If his niece is – or was – one of *them*, what is the chance that he is, too? That's a very important question, and I have to know the answer. An educated guess, as reasoned as you can make it. Just what, in your opinion, are the chances that Itaguari himself is a clandestine member of the terrorists?'

The Minister said promptly: 'None at all, I'm quite sure of it.'

'Till I told you differently,' Meyers said, 'you would have been equally sure about Estrella.'

'No,' the Minister was quite emphatic, 'there are reasons which assure me that he is not.'

'Ah.' It was Colonel Tobin. He said gently: 'And those reasons are . . . ?'

The Minister squirmed. He said, hesitantly: 'I wonder if you would not insist on an answer to that question? Will you not take my assurance that there are good reasons? State secrets, if you like to regard them as that?'

'No,' Colonel Tobin said. 'Decidedly, no.'

He waited, and they all looked at him, and Colonel Tobin said at last, impatiently: 'Is it necessary for me to remind you of your Prime Minister's instructions to you?'

'No, I suppose not.' The Minister hesitated again, and said at last, sighing: 'They call them the Death Squads, in Rio de Janeiro. You must have heard of them.'

The Colonel said softly: 'Ah, so that's it . . . '

For a moment, nobody else spoke. There was no need for comment. The Death Squads earned their own little headlines in the papers two, three, sometimes more times every week:

' . . . A, a suspected terrorist, was found stabbed to death in Rua Nascimento this morning . . . '

' . . . B, known to have participated in the bomb attack on the German Consulate last Friday, was found dead in Rua Dias Ferreira during the night . . . '

' . . . C, one of the chief suspects in last week's murder of three

61

police officers, was found stabbed to death in Ipanema early this morning . . .'

' . . . . D and E, who have been on the most-wanted list put out by the Police for the last three months, were discovered late last night in a culvert on Morro dos Cabritos. Both had been stabbed to death . . .'

The Minister said sadly: 'I'm afraid there is very definite evidence that Colonel Itaguari is quite closely connected with the infamous Death Squads.'

Rick Meyers said sharply: 'How definite?'

The Minister shrugged: 'In the higher echelons of his Department, it is no secret at all. He has told me of it himself.'

'And why, then, has nothing ever been done about it?'

It was his whole country that was under attack now. The Minister sat straight in his chair and said, speaking very clearly so that they would understand exactly how he felt about it:

'It is known that the Death Squads are made up of police and army officers who have lost patience with the rather slow and laborious methods of constitutional justice. Their first killing . . . their first murder, occurred six years ago, when Carlo Redondo, who had without a doubt murdered no less than six policemen, was acquitted for lack of direct evidence by a judge whose deference to the niceties of the law was, to say the least of it . . . ' he groped for the right word, and said at last; 'finicky. The case against Redondo was clear-cut. Two of his murders were seen by witnesses of unimpeachable integrity. He was acquitted because of an error, a clerical error, in the wording of the arrest warrant, and on his release, he boasted to the Press – boasted, mark you! – that he would continue what he called the good work he had begun, and that next time he would take care not to be caught. He went underground immediately, of course. And three nights later, he was found murdered. It was the first . . . execution by the Death Squads. As we all know, there have since been many, many others. No one can approve of them, but . . . '

He shrugged broadly. 'Shall I say that some of us sleep better after known assassins are put decisively out of business? And so . . . even though some of us know at least a few of the Squad members . . . we do not prosecute them as effectively as perhaps we should.' He felt that it was not a very good argument, and he added hastily: 'And of course, we have never yet been able to find any direct evidence against any single one of them. Determined as we are to use only constitutional means in our fight against terrorism, we can hardly apply unconstitutional methods against those who also fight it, but unconstitutionally.' He said, deprecatingly, 'Colonel Itaguari, and Captain da Costa – the late Captain da Costa – they were the two men who really led the Death Squads.'

Colonel Tobin thought about it for a while. He said finally: 'Well, we're all agreed that it's a pretty lousy business, you can't fight terror with more terror, we all know that, and when we get the business of the Xiristas cleared up, perhaps the government will be moved to put its foot down a little more firmly. I'll have a word with the Prime Minister about Itaguari, but meanwhile, we've got other business on our hands.'

He sipped his drink for a while, leaning back in his chair and thinking. The sun was high in the sky now, the brilliance reflected up on to the bamboo roof from the broad water below them. Across the open verandah he could see the posted sentries, the Minister's own military bodyguard patrolling in pairs, their rifles on their shoulders, marching stiffly; and his own three men wandering up and down in apparent aimlessness, constantly on the move, constantly changing direction, constantly alert for the slightest sound or scent of any alien intruder.

At last he said: 'All right, and that brings us to the one thing left that you have to know about.' He turned to Betty de Haas: 'You have the chart ready?'

She left her seat and spread out a map of Rio de Janeiro on the table in front of the Minister, standing beside him, very close, so close he could smell her perfume. He was tempted to grope with his left hand, and fought the impulse nobly. She touched at the map with the tip of her silver pencil, and her voice was low, and soft, and very feminine.

She said: 'Here, the Presidential summer home. Here, the Headquarters of the National Guard. Here, the residence of the Minister for Land Affairs. The American Embassy, the German Embassy . . . here, the Parliament Building. Here, the three main plants of the Electricity and Water Board, here and here, the two main television and radio stations . . . ' She went back over them one by one, counting them out: 'Eleven crucial buildings. Each one is mined, and scheduled for destruction. Under the Presidential Palace alone there are four hundred pounds of high explosive. Under the National Guard Building, two hundred and forty. Under the house of the Minister for Land Affairs, there's only eighty pounds, but it's under the floor of the Conference Room. All the charges have been wired, and are ready for detonation.

They'll be fired electronically by UHF radio signal, when Juan Xira is ready. The destruction of these buildings will be the signal for the general uprising. Now . . . '

The Minister was staring at her in shock.

Calmly, she spread out a map of Brazil, and moved her pencil around: 'Manaus, Belem, the Blue Mountain in the Mato Grosso on the Jaqui River in the Rio Grande do Sul, and in the Minas Gerais only four hundred miles from Rio itself, the five armies that Xira has collected together have been openly showing themselves, trying to tempt your armies to come after them, trying to disperse your forces. But for the past two weeks they've all been moving out, discreetly, and they are all now in the Tapajos area.'

The Minister could hardly restrain himself. He said, smiling: 'No, my dear young lady, that's not true. At least, not entirely so. Only the night before last, the whole of the southern slope of the Blue Mountain was covered with the Xirista camp fires, a thousand men, at least . . . '

'Four men,' Betty de Haas said. 'Four men, left behind specifically to keep those fires burning, to fire off a machine-gun or two once in a while. There were fourteen hundred men there two weeks ago. Now they are all in Tapajos.'

'Oh.'

Rick said, taking over: 'Twenty-four hours before the signal is given, the Tapajos army starts to move. And twenty-four hours *after* the signal, Juan Xira takes over the government. That is their schedule. One day before, and one day after D-Day. From then on in . . . mass executions every day, a few choice parties reserved for spectacular trials, secession from the Organisation of American States . . . and war against Bolivia.'

His shock had changed to horror. He looked from Rick to the Colonel and said, stuttering:

'D-Day? For God's sake . . . And when is that?'

Rick Meyers said cheerfully: 'That's what we hope to find out, Minister. All we know right now is that it's going to be very, very soon.'

CHAPTER SIX

RIO DE JANEIRO
Co-ordinates: 22.54S: 43.14W

He could have been a clerical assistant at the Post Office, or perhaps a minor accountant from one of the big stores; he was a thin and undernourished kind of man, perhaps forty years old, with a worried, studious look about him. It was only when he took off the steel-rimmed glasses that you could see the fire of fanaticism that constantly burned in his eyes.

And it was only when he began to speak that you could understand the immense fascination that he had for so many of the people. Then, he would begin quietly appealing to the reason of his listeners; and he would slowly, surely, twist them around to his way of thinking with rhetoric and argument that seemed, for the moment at least, utterly plausible. And once, his typewriter had been his most dangerous weapon.

But not any more. Now he had discovered that he could kill as easily as the rest of them – and more venomously.

The car was parked in the shadows of the plane trees along the Rio Branco, just across the street from the Municipal Theatre. From an open doorway, he could hear the faint sound of the music coming from inside there, and he looked further down the street and saw the two taxicabs waiting, four men in each of them. A police car passed slowly by, prowling, and one of the cabs glided away, drove round the block, and came back again. The prowl car passed his own, and he grinned at the two policemen in it and stuck up his thumb in a friendly gesture; it passed on.

He looked at his watch; the third car was late, and he swung round in his seat to stare through the back window, waiting for it, and when at last it came round the corner and parked just behind him, he sat back again and waited.

They were all in position now: four cars, eleven men, six submachine guns, five pistols, and four hand grenades on the seat beside him in his own car.

He said to the driver: 'Turn the engine over, let it run for a few minutes.'

The driver nodded and started the car, then switched off again a few moments later.

The sound of the music there had stopped now, and the audience was clapping, cheering, some of them beginning to move out. He saw the black limousine of the Ambassador pull in to the curb and stop, saw the driver throw away his cigarette, saw the policeman sitting beside him in the light of the tall street lamp.

He switched on the walkie-talkie, and said quietly: 'Jao? You stay right behind me, on my tail, you understand?'

Jao was a kid, not much more than sixteen years old, but he was the best marksman in the group, a boy devoid of any fear at all, three murders to his credit already. He stuttered; he always did when he was excited: 'B-bem, b-bem, comprehendo . . . '

The policeman in the Ambassador's car had climbed down and was holding the door to the rear compartment open, and then the Ambassador himself was there, chatting amiably with his lady, a middle-aged matron in a long grey gown that gleamed in the sulphurous lights. Together, they climbed into the limousine, and it glided away, moving slowly through the crowds.

The crowds were good, but it was too light here. A block and a half further down, where the truck would be waiting . . . he wondered for a moment if perhaps he should have been in the truck himself, and then decided that Mostero could handle it well enough on his own, a simple job for a simple man.

He spoke into the radio again: 'Julava? Any minute now, get ready.' Julava was on the roof of the theatre, waiting with the shotgun, the four crucial street lights well within his range.

He said to the driver: 'Go . . . ' and the car moved off, close on the Ambassador's tail, easing its way through the crowds that were streaming out of the doors. The limousine was a hundred feet ahead of him now, and one of the taxis moved in behind it, ahead of him, and he pulled in a little tighter and watched the other taxi pull in behind him.

And then, at the corner, the truck shot out into the street, a ten-ton dump truck stolen an hour ago from the roadbuilders along the Rua Dantas. Somehow, with less than a hundred yards to go, Mostero had reached a speed of more than forty miles an hour, and at the moment of impact he swung the wheel over hard and pushed the limousine over the curb and on to the grass and the flowers of the garden that ran down the center of the street.

He leaped out of the car, the four hand-grenades ready, and saw that the two taxis had pulled into their proper positions and were disgorging the gunmen; he found time to approve of their timing, of the way they moved in precise concord with one another, three of the men with their Schmeissers taking the front, three more to the rear, all facing outwards and holding their weapons on the crowd, the women among them screaming, the men – this too was the pattern of their lives – running for cover before the firing would start.

He heard the blast of the shotgun high above his head, then another, and another, and another, and he saw the street lights shatter, and now there was only the light from the lamps further down the road.

It was time for the diversion.

He crouched down behind the big square steel garbage container, and hurled the first of his grenades back into the crowd at the doors of the theater. He counted the seconds for the explosion, and hurled another, listening to the screams of the wounded and enjoying them. Behind him he heard the two pistol shots that meant, he knew, the death of the chauffeur and the bodyguard, heard the sudden burst of machine-gun fire that meant, no doubt, that one of the men had seen the police car racing in. He could see it himself out of the corner of his eye; it crashed into the wall and no one moved out of it.

And now, the black taxi was racing off, its tires burning, Mostero climbing aboard as it swung past him and momentarily skidded to an abrupt stop, then took off again, fast. The other men were getting back into their own taxi, and he waited for them to drive off in the opposite direction, and he took one quick look around and threw his last but one grenade to discourage any close approach, keeping the final one in reserve, as he always did, for emergencies. He walked over to the crashed police car, taking his time now, knowing that there was one thing left to do, and one thing only.

He flung open its doors, tugging at it to get it free, and looked inside. One of the policemen there was dead, the other wounded, a swathe of bullets across his hips and the blood still pumping out. He reached over calmly and took their revolvers, and he took the wounded policeman by the hair and shook him, and put his face in very close and said: 'Can you hear me? Before you die, tell them that Juan Xira is back. You understand me? Juan Xira.' He said, mocking: 'They know the name.'

He dragged the man out and dropped him on the asphalt, and

saw that he would live for a while, and kicked him in the face and walked away. He saw five, six, seven bodies lying near the doors of the great yellow stone building, saw a group of frightened people huddled in the doorway, saw the faces staring at him from half-opened windows. The car was circling round, its rear door open, and he got inside it and said calmly to the driver: 'All right, you know where to go. Go there.'

The clock on the Cathedral tower was striking the quarter-hour; the whole operation had taken two and a half minutes.

The Ambassador had been badly hurt. Someone had driven a rifle-butt into his face and had cracked his jaw, and he was trying to work the muscles to ease the pain.

He said to the man who was tying his arms behind his back: 'Could I perhaps have a glass of water? Please?' It was hard to sound the sibilants. His arms were wrenched painfully back over the top of the wooden chair, the thumbs being tightly tied together. His eyes were blindfolded, and he could smell the ripe scent of *feijoa* cooking somewhere. A woman's voice said: 'The feet, too, tie the feet,' and he felt hands grabbing at his ankles and roping them to the legs of the chair.

He heard the door open and close, heard the soft pad of rope-soled shoes, and then the bandage was ripped off his face and the light was blinding him.

He looked around the room; six, seven men, all armed with submachine guns, one of them at the window with the edge of the canvas drape in his hand, staring down on to the street outside.

The man who had pulled away the bandage was peering into his eyes, a slight, undernourished man with steel-rimmed glasses and dark, intelligent eyes. He said: 'You know who I am, Senhor Ambassador?'

The Ambassador nodded. He said steadily: 'I know who you are, I've seen your photograph, many times. Juan Xira.'

'Good. I am told you speak excellent Portuguese.'

'Yes. Yes, I do.'

Xira said: 'I have a paper for you to sign, a demand to the government for certain conditions for your release. Are you prepared to sign it, without any coercion?'

The Ambassador looked at him in the face and said: 'You murdered my chauffeur, you murdered the policeman who was with him, is it your intention to murder me too?'

Xira shook his head, the answer to a question that was only

68

academic. He said frankly: 'No, that won't be necessary. You are far more useful to us alive.'

'Three days ago, you kidnapped General Faleira. A week before that you kidnapped the first secretary of the Universal Aid Society. Where are they now? Where are all the others?'

The woman whose voice he had heard moved into his line of vision, coming from behind him and saying mockingly: 'He's afraid they're dead.'

She was a very young girl, perhaps only sixteen or seventeen years old, with thick-lensed glasses and long, untidy hair. The man said to her: 'They're all afraid to die, Gloria. That's what makes them different from us, isn't it?' She laughed, and found an apple and started munching on it.

Juan Xira turned back to the Ambassador. His voice was gentle, the voice of a scholar explaining a simple point to an obtuse student:

'Let me assure you, we need our hostages alive. If they were marked for execution, they would have been killed, not kidnapped, can't you understand that?'

'The lady who was with me . . . what happened to her?'

Xira shrugged: 'Frankly, I do not know. I saw her running away. Perhaps she escaped, perhaps she was killed. I don't think it matters very much. We'll know in the morning, won't we, when the papers carry the story. Who was she?'

The Ambassador said coldly: 'And that doesn't matter either, does it?'

'Well, I won't insist.'

Xira went to the table and opened a drawer, and pulled out a sheet of paper. He stood there for a while, studying it carefully, and lit a cigarette and let the blue smoke curl up over his face, then he perched himself on the edge of the table and said: 'What about the list?'

One of the men answered him: 'Santarem has it, all the names you wanted.'

'And Cheleiros?'

'No. We're still not sure about her. We still don't think they took her; no one at Police Headquarters knows anything about that.'

Xira nodded absently; he was worried. He drew on his cigarette and stared at it, the sheet of paper held loosely in his hand. 'I don't like the Cheleiros business, I don't know who took her or why. I want someone to track her down, I want her found and eliminated, she's a danger to us.' He went back to reading the

69

paper again, and when he had finished, he looked at the Ambassador and said: 'I'll tell you the gist of it, and you can sign it.'

'No. Let me see it.'

Xira got down off the table and moved over, and hit him once, not very hard, across the face, and said: 'While you are with us, you have no authority whatsoever. You give no orders, you understand?' He turned to one of the men: 'Untie his hands.'

He went back then, and sat on the table again, and began to read, nonetheless:

'Personal to the Prime Minister, from Juan Xira, Leader of the Revolutionary Committee of Liberation. In exchange for the life of Ambassador Steuben, I submit the following demands:

ONE: The immediate release of all the prisoners at present held in the prison of Sao Paulo, whose names are appended hereto.

TWO: Immediate publication in the Jornal do Brasil *of the Revolutionary Manifesto already in your possession.*

THREE: Payment of the sum of ten million cruzeiros to us at such time and under such conditions as shall be specified in our next communication.

FOUR: The immediate removal from office, and exile to a country of your choice but not on the Continent of South America, of Colonel Itaguari, Head of the Secret Police.

FIVE: Immediate withdrawal of all troops in the Manous–Belem–Gurupa area of the Amazon Delta. None of these demands is negotiable. Ambassador Steuben is in good health, and is aware of these demands.'

He looked at Steuben and said, almost apologetically: 'As a diplomat, you will understand that they really are negotiable, but we have to say that, don't we? If they agreed to half of these demands, we'll be quite satisfied and you'll be released. There's one more paragraph, a personal note from you. I'll read it to you.'

He went on, reading, his voice very clear and precise:

'I, Ambassador Steuben, have read and understood the foregoing, and in fear of my life I beg you to accede at once to these demands. I have been told that I will be killed if the conditions are not met, and I publicly and earnestly entreat the government of Brazil to take note of the incalculable harm that my execution would cause to the currently favorable re-

70

lationship between our two countries. Signed, Heinrich Steuben, Ambassador.'

He said: 'Well, there it is. Are you going to sign it? I assure you, it's in your own interest to do so.'

The blood was beginning to circulate in his arms again, but the pain in his jaw was excruciating. He took a deep breath and fought back the fear, and said clearly: 'No, I will not. Obviously, I cannot. That's all there is to it.'

Xira was perched up on the edge of the table, his legs dangling, an air of appalling nonchalance about him. He said, almost disinterestedly: 'Your private residence has been mined. There are a hundred and fifty kilos of high explosive in your cellars . . . ' He laughed shortly and said: 'In the corner where you have stored those cases of . . . ' He turned to the man by the window. 'What was it? Schnapps?'

'Yes, eight cases, from Hamburg.'

He turned back to Steuben, and shrugged broadly: 'You see, I'm not trying to fool you. If they're detonated, the interior walls, I am told, will collapse. I'm also told that your sister is there, your two children, and four of your staff. So you see, the choice is up to you. I need your signature, Ambassador. I've detected a hardening of the government attitude, and I want it back on its previously even keel once more. So . . . ?'

The Ambassador said: 'Give me the paper. I'll sign it.'

Someone gave him a book to hold on his knee while he signed, and Xira examined the signature carefully. He found a manila envelope in the drawer, and carefully sealed it, and handed it to the man at the window and said: 'Get this over to the *Jornal do Brasil*, and then telephone police headquarters and tell them it's there. Give me your rifle, we'll be leaving here shortly.'

The man nodded, handed over the carbine, took the envelope, and went out. Someone was tying the Ambassador's hands behind his back again; it was the young woman they had called Gloria, and he could smell the ripe scent of her apple as she held it in her mouth.

He saw that Xira was staring at him, a thoughtful, almost worried look on his face, as though some problem were disturbing him. He said at last, very slowly, an academic question: 'Your country has been supplying arms to Bolivia for a long time now, and yet they've suddenly, quietly, stopped deliveries. Why is that?'

The Ambassador said steadily: 'We found out that they were

71

being passed on to you, Senhor Xira. My country has no wish to support the revolutionaries in South America. Our agreements are only with legally-constituted governments.'

'Yes. Yes, that's what I thought. But we don't need the Bolivian arms any more now. We don't even need you any more.'

He looked at the girl and jerked his head at her, and the Ambassador felt her soft hand on his forehead, almost a caress, and then her hand was in his hair, grabbing it and pulling his head sharply back. He strained to turn and see what she was doing, but he could not.

He saw Xira lighting a fresh cigarette, watching him, and then there was a thin cord at his throat, and the girl was tying it at the nape of his neck. He felt her pull the ends tight, and tighter still, and he tried to gasp for breath and could not find any. And then, the bright colors were changing as she tugged harder and secured the knot, and the room began to spin around him, and he struggled and upset the chair and fell with it to the floor, and the last thing he was conscious of was those shining steel spectacles over the murderous eyes, and then, he died.

Xira watched him for a while, and then slipped off the table again and walked to the door, and said to no one in particular: 'He mustn't be found. Under no circumstances must he be found. And I want everyone out of here before daylight.'

He went out and closed the door behind him.

On the street, he found the bicycle that had been left there for him, and as he mounted it he heard a movement at his side, and a shadow moved out of the doorway there.

He peered and said: 'Braga? Is that you?'

'Yes. Jorge Braga. How is it, Juan?'

'Everything is well. What are you doing here?'

'Watching. Arrifana told me to watch.'

'Ah yes, Arrifana. Good. You are a good man, Braga.'

'Where will you go now?'

Xira shrugged; but his eyes were piercing: 'Where will I go? Only God and Xira know where I go, and there is no God, so only Xira knows. Good-night, Braga.'

'Good-night, Juan.'

Xira silently pedalled off in the direction of the *favella* where he would be spending the remainder of the night, an animal, hiding in the darkness.

CHAPTER SEVEN

RIO DE JANEIRO
Co-ordinates: 22.52S: 43.15W.

Confolens was there to meet him in Rio, dapper and elegant as always, in a tan suit of raw silk with a yellow silk ascot round his throat, standing slim and straight in the hot sun, his white hair shining, an impossibly cool and unflustered look about him. He said: 'Paul . . . how was the trip?'

The trip was too damn long, Paul was thinking, it takes forever to cross this country. He said: 'Fine, I caught up on my sleep, how's the lady?'

'The lady is well, and . . . quite astounding.'

'And I hope she's well under wraps; they'll be busting a gut trying to find her now. Rick tells me she's cooperating very well with us, and I must say . . . that alarms me a trifle.'

'Talk to her, Paul. You might change your mind. I'm not easily fooled, you know that.'

'Have you moved her?'

'Yes, of course, as soon as we got your word. I've got her on a rented yacht . . .'

Paul said sharply: 'Outside the harbor?'

Confolens smiled. 'Yes, of course, and it's the fastest boat on the whole of the coast, nothing can catch it if we have to run. We can be outside territorial waters in twelve minutes, and I've moved a three-pounder on board. I don't imagine we'll ever have to use it, but Rick says there's a small group of ex-naval officers who have secretly joined the Xiristas, and they might have access to a sea-going craft. We just might have to fight them.'

'I know. Four of them, possibly five, the men who were fired last year for holding back on their sailors' wages; we've got our eye on them. But the Navy's pretty solidly on the side of the government, and I don't think they'll want to tangle. Hold it.'

He walked over to the news-stand and bought a paper, the *Jornal do Brasil*, and stood frowning at it, reading the headline and worrying. He said: 'Steuben . . . what would they want with

73

him, I wonder? You know about it?'

Confolens nodded. 'Yes. I'll tell you about it in the car.'

They moved out on to the street, and found Cass Fragonard waiting for them in a Willys, and drove down to the beach at Ipanema where Manuel would be waiting with the outboard to take them out to the yacht.

Paul said: 'All right, what about the Ambassador?'

Confolens sighed; Paul wasn't going to like it a bit. He said: 'Ambassador Steuben, he was at the theatre last night in spite of the warning we'd passed on to him. He'd given the police an assurance that he wouldn't leave his residence for the next two weeks, because it was known something was afoot. But he changed his mind, decided at the last minute to attend the Fine Arts Concert, didn't tell a soul he was going. And they were waiting for him. Seven people killed, eighteen wounded, half of them critically, with machine gun fire and hand grenades.'

Reading, frowning, Paul said: 'The woman with him. Who was she?'

'Nicola has been down at Police Headquarters all morning, trying to find that out; we should know later on this afternoon. On the surface, it appears that she was a casual acquaintance of the Ambassador who turned up at his house during the afternoon on what the servants said was a friendly call. That's when the Ambassador changed his mind. The chances are, it was she who persuaded him, and if so . . . ' he shrugged. 'They are all around us, aren't they?'

'We'd better find out where they've got him. And fast.'

Confolens said gently: 'Too late, Paul. They killed him.' Paul said nothing. Confolens went on: 'Braga was almost, but not quite there when it happened. Jorge Braga, he's a good man, but I don't know how much longer his cover is going to hold out, he's treading on thin ice already.'

'Braga has to stay put, we need him. Go on.'

'The press has been told that Steuben is still alive, but it seems that Xira had him strangled as soon as he'd got to sign a plea that he wanted circulated.' He shrugged. 'They'll make sure the body is well hidden, keep up the pretense that he's still a hostage, and hope that the government will give in to them.' He added sourly: 'Again.'

'But we know, I take it, where the body is?'

'We know. Braga again. It's in a trunk up in the forest at Corcovado. I'm just waiting for the okay from you to let the police in on the secret.'

'You seem pretty sure that Xira himself did this, that he's in town?'

'Yes. Braga saw him, spoke to him.'

Paul said harshly: 'And?'

For a moment, Confolens did not answer. He stared out of the window at the bright blue sea, the dark, sun-tanned bodies packed tightly on the beach, the young men playing *futbal* and the girls sunning themselves by the bright, colored umbrellas, and said at last:

'Yes, I know what you're thinking. It's the first time Xira has ever been seen by one of our men, and maybe, just possibly, Braga could have done something about it. But you said yourself, we're not ready yet, the time isn't ripe. We've got to get all of them together. And Braga is the only hope we have got of getting close to Xira, of getting him where we want him *when* we want him. They've accepted him, his cover has stood up under the closest possible scrutiny. If he'd acted in any way last night he would have blown it wide open.' He hesitated. 'It's the Faleira case all over again. Maybe I could have saved Faleira if I'd broken a few rules, and maybe Braga could have saved Steuben, I just don't know. But I do know that if we lose our cover . . . you've always hammered that home, and so has Bramble, and so has the Colonel.'

'Yes, and we mustn't forget. It's hard, sometimes, to wait. But that's what war is, and this is just that . . . a war.'

Confolens said: 'That's the launch there now.'

They crossed over the beach and jumped aboard the motor-boat, and Manuel took them far out over the silver-blue sea to the yacht riding quietly at anchor a mile and a half offshore. And there, sitting placidly and undisturbed by her confinement, was Estrella Cheleiros.

Paul could not stop his heart from beating faster when he looked at her. She turned her head slowly and gazed, rather than looked at him, a distant, almost absent look in her lovely eyes, as though her thoughts were very far away indeed. The movement was slow and steady, a gentle turning of the head so that the shoulders remained exactly as they were before, half-turned to him. She was toying with a diamond pin that had come from her hair, hair that was loose now, and flowing down over her shoulders, down the bodice of her white gown and right down to the waist; he thought he'd never seen a lovelier woman before.

He jumped lightly on to the deck and approached her, and said, smiling: 'My name is Paul Tobin, Senhora. I suppose you could call me your principal jailor. Have they been treating you well?'

She held out her hand to him, the knuckles uppermost, a gesture she might make to a friend presented to her. He took it and held it briefly, then let it drop again. She said: 'Well enough, Senhor Tobin, under the circumstances. But . . . if you propose keeping me much longer, I shall need some clothes.'

Confolens said swiftly: 'Nicola, she's bringing some this evening.'

'Good.'

Paul pulled up a chair and sat down in front of her, leaning in towards her and not taking his eyes off hers. He said: 'I understand you're well aware of what's been happening, is that so?'

'I know that I was drugged and asked a lot of questions. I'm not at all sure what they all were.'

His eyes dropped to her waist; he could easily have encircled it with his hands. The white gown was slit down the front, very low, her breasts small and pointed like a child's.

He nodded. 'And I understand you've told us a lot of things about your friends, the Xiristas.' He gestured at her with the file that Bramble had given him. 'Quite a lot here, and quite a lot more I hope to learn from you. Senhor Confolens here seems to think you might be regretting your allegiance to them.'

'Senhor Confolens told me that Juan Xira had ordered my execution.' She shuddered.

'Yes, that's true. What is open to doubt is whether you believe it to be true or not, whether you perhaps think we are merely pulling the wool over your eyes in the hope of getting your co-operation. Was Xira your friend?'

'No. He was . . . our leader.'

He wondered if he should remind her of what they had done to the General, or would Confolens have kept a discreet silence about that?

He looked at Confolens and said: 'I take it you've kept the newspapers away from her?'

'Yes. Yes, of course.'

The faint rebuke in his tone told him what he wanted to know; she hadn't heard about Faleira's mutilation. He decided to say nothing about it. He said instead: 'Suppose you tell me when and how you first met Juan Xira. And would you like something to drink?'

'No, thank you.' She hesitated. 'I'd like to walk around a little, if I may?'

He was surprised, and hurt. 'Of course you may! They haven't tried to keep you sitting here all the time, have they?'

'No. Only . . . ' Her eyes started to the man sitting on the edge of the rail at the prow, a rifle across his knees, and Paul said irritably:

'He is not here to harm you, he's there to keep watch, to see that no one approaches us; your late friends are not going to give you up just because you've dropped out of sight. They'll be searching the town for you, remember that, remember that you're only safe with us.' He knew that his tone was harsh, and he smiled quickly and said: 'And if there's anything you want, anything at all except your freedom, please ask for it, we'll do what we can. All right?'

'Yes. Yes, of course.'

He matched his pace to hers, and they strolled up and down together, almost like two lovers on a cruise. He watched her covertly, admiring the way she moved, a slow, feline, deliberate, motion of her hips, her head thrown slightly back, her neck long and white and beautiful, the black hair cascading.

He said, making conversation, putting her at ease: 'Is your cabin comfortable? Do you have everything you need?'

'Oh, yes, more or less. I know this yacht, it used to belong to the American who owns the Beeswax Company. We used to go fishing sometimes, it's very fast. Is that why . . . ?'

'Yes. In case your friends find out you're here.'

'And if they do . . . ' she stopped her pacing and turned to look at him. 'If they attack you, what would happen to me?'

He could detect the fear in her voice. He put a hand on her arm and said quickly: 'Nothing at all. We have no intention of saving you from them by killing you, if that's what you're afraid of. If they find us . . . I promise you, one way or another, you'll be safe.'

His hand was still on her arm, the touch of her flesh warm, and she turned away from him and looked out over the sea, and said: 'No one will tell me who you are, and I've been wondering. You're an American, aren't you?'

'No, English,' he said drily, 'the next best thing. We've been engaged by the Brazilian Government to help them out with the Xiristas. Juan Xira is getting a little tough for them to handle. We're experts in that sort of thing. How well do you know him?'

She had resumed her pacing. 'Xira? Oh, two years, I suppose, a little more perhaps. He was in prison, and he escaped, and he came to my house to see . . . I suppose she was his girl, I don't know. A friend, at least; one of my servants. I found him in the stables in a corner of the grounds; I'd gone there to see one of the horses who was sick, and . . . well, he was there, with the girl who looks after the dogs, and he'd been beaten terribly, by the police it seems, I never saw a man before who'd been beaten like that, it was terrible. He said he'd killed one of the guards, and that others had attacked him like a pack of hounds, but he'd got away and . . . '

She broke off and turned to look again across the water at the distant beach, and said: 'If you kill one man, it makes sense that his friends will lose their temper and beat you to within an inch of your life, but even so . . . there was something about him, something . . . wretched. I felt sorry for him, and when the girl begged me, with tears in her eyes, to say nothing about it, I just . . . forgot the whole incident, pretended it had never happened. And then, ten days later, I found him in my room one night. He'd climbed in through the window, like a common burglar, and I thought the girl had helped him, because she handles the dogs, you understand? But all he wanted was to thank me. He couldn't understand why I hadn't given him away, I couldn't even understand it myself, and he spoke to me at great length, telling me of the evils this country has fallen in to. Oh, I know, he's a Communist, isn't he? And they don't always talk sense, but nonetheless I began to believe at least some of what he told me. He knew that Colonel Itaguari was my uncle, and he told me about some of the things that happen in the cells at the prison . . . I don't know whether they are true or not, but at the time, I believed him. He was so . . . so eloquent.' She looked up at him, not at all sure of herself. 'Are those things true?'

Paul said heavily: 'There's a great deal of evil on both sides, I'm afraid. And while there's revolution and counter-revolution, they won't stop. They'll stop when the country reaches the kind of stability it's been striving for ever since 1964. That was a revolution too, you remember. They can't go on forever. And it's getting better, more enlightened, all the time. This is why we agreed to help a government whose record is not exactly blameless. Not blameless, but getting better month by month. They are trying, and we are trying to help them. If Juan Xira's revolution succeeds . . . did you know that he has a list of over two thousand officials marked for execution? Without trials?'

She shook her head and said quietly: 'No, I did not know that.'

He could not believe that her conversion had been so complete. And yet . . . he was thinking: If someone ordered *my* execution, I'd hit back so damned hard . . . why should I deny her the same spirit?

He said, prompting her: 'But you and Xira became quite close?' He hesitated, sensing the indelicacy. 'How close?'

She said, smiling: 'Oh, he wasn't my lover, if that's what you mean. He had a sister, a woman named Juanita Xira, much older than he is, and she disappeared, and he thought she'd been arrested by the Security Police. He wanted me to find out from my uncle, and somehow . . . there was always the memory of that other girl, in tears over him, so I made a few inquiries and found out that she'd been killed. An accident, they said. I was never able to find out exactly what happened. He almost went into shock when I told him. And then, from time to time I helped him, in little ways. Once, I warned him when my uncle's men were on their way to seize him; they'd found out where he was hiding, and after that . . . it seemed natural that I should help him more and more. Until one day, quite recently, he asked me for some information about the military, a brigade of men who were sent into the field somewhere up in the Amazon area, the River Tapajos I think it was. He said he wanted to know where they were going so that he could move his men out of the area. Instead . . he fought them. They were all taken prisoner, and I heard that some of the officers were just . . . murdered.'

'Not just the officers. All of them.'

Her face was white as she stared at him. He said brutally: 'Two hundred and eighty men, there's a mass grave if you'd like to see it, in what used to be known as Xirista Camp Four. He personally ordered their execution.' It was time to hit her harder, and he said: 'I'm told you move a great deal among the members of the diplomatic corps. Tell me about Ambassador Steuben.'

'Heinrich Steuben? He is a charming man, a dear friend. A good man too. Why do you ask?'

Paul said: 'Your dear friend Xira murdered him last night. The *Jornal* carries a demand from the terrorists this morning, another of their demands for money, for the publication of their manifesto, for a lot of other things as well. Xira has promised that if the government accedes to his demands, Steuben will be released, unharmed. And he has already dumped his hostage's body in a trunk on the slopes of Corcovado. So much for your persuasive friend Xira.'

Her hands were at her face, whiter than ever before. He saw her shudder, and then she was in tears. He put his arm around her waist and said: 'Tears won't help him, but I wanted you to know. I wanted you to know the kind of people you've been mixed up with.'

They found a white-painted bench and sat together on it, feeling the gentle rocking of the yacht on the water, a lullaby. He said at last, not sure just why he wanted to know, to hear it from her: 'Tell me about General Faleira. Your relationship with him.' He shrugged. 'Oh, I know he is your lover, but . . . I want to know about the man, how you feel about him. Do you love him?'

'He is very good to me.'

'That wasn't the question.'

'I'm sure he loves me very dearly.'

'And you?'

'No. Not really. But he's so . . . so good, and kind, and . . . yes, I suppose I must say it. Generous. We get on so very well together, we understand each other. We never fight. About anything.'

'And is that your idea of what love is? That you don't ever fight?'

'No. I told you, I do not truly love him, I am comfortable with him.'

What would she have been had she never met the General? Surely she was one of the most beautiful women in all Brazil – the whole of the country would have been at her feet! Thousands of men who must have swarmed around her, and yet, she had chosen the General, a brave and honorable man, but a man with a fearsome reputation, and old enough to be her grandfather. He wondered if the key to her character was here, somewhere, tucked away for him to find if he probed hard enough.

But then – did it really *matter*? Wasn't it enough that she was his prisoner, that she could provide at least some of the information they needed about that elusive enemy? He thought again about Jorge Braga, wondered if perhaps he should have taken some sort of action when he found himself face to face with Xira, the man they had already spent three months hunting down . . . no, Confolens was right, as he always was; the time was not yet; there were too many other problems to be solved first. Not least of them – that equally elusive army that was no longer a rabble, but a highly-organised force, fighting with modern weapons supplied by the cynical proponents of its opposing political philosophy.

He thought again about the Major back there in the swamps, Major Borja de Quemada. Were their sources now strong enough, with Borja up north and Estrella here in the south? He thought perhaps they were . . .

They had resumed their strolling, walking slowly side by side, with the deep blue water shimmering below them. She had taken off her shoes, and was walking barefoot; in the long evening gown, with the heat of the sun around them, it gave her a pagan look that he admired; but that look of hers made him restless.

He said: 'In those days, how did you get in touch with Juan Xira? Or did he always come to you?'

'No. I simply told my maid I had a message for him. She is a runner for them, a messenger.'

'And she's still with you?'

'Yes. Her name is Maria Josinara, she lives at my house in Sao Sebastiao.'

'Then I take it she'd know where to find Xira? At any given time?'

'No. She could get a message to him, but where to find him . . . no one ever knows where he is. He comes, and he goes, a very secretive man.'

And then Confolens was there, moving in quickly and saying: 'I think it might be wiser if you two stay on this side of the boat. We're being watched.' He was smiling, and the high-powered naval glasses were in his hand. He handed them to Paul and said: 'Why don't you go below and take a look. The outboard between us and the shore – it's been there for the last five minutes. I haven't shown myself, and I don't think either of you has been seen, but . . . why don't you take a look?'

They hurried down the companionway together, the three of them, and went to the forward cabin. Paul opened the shutters on the shore side a little and looked out through the glasses. In a moment, he said: 'Yes indeed, he's watching us through his binoculars, not very covertly, one man alone, a good little boat.'

Confolens said: 'And he's one of *them*.'

'Are you sure of that?'

'Oh yes, quite sure. The last time I saw him, he was on the beach at Copacabana, selling pineapples to the late lamented Captain da Costa.'

'Ah yes, I saw the report. Did you ever find out what it was that killed the Captain?'

'We did indeed. I dropped a hint to the senior social columnist of the *Jornal do Brasil*, and she passed it on to the proper authorities. He died of a heavy dose of arsenic. They even found a slice of pineapple lying on the beach, and a dead dog, too, that had nibbled at it. And I owe her, sooner or later, the story.'

Paul said, watching: 'One man, alone. How long has he been there?'

'Manuel spotted him five minutes ago.'

'All right, lower a boat, will you do that? On the starboard side, offshore. Get Estrella aboard it, and all the others. How many people have we on board?'

Confolens was puzzled. 'Seven, all told.'

'Everybody aboard the boat except you and me. Have it cast off now and wait for us.'

'All right.' He went out and Paul squirmed round on a padded bench and made himself comfortable, and kept the glasses to his eyes and waited.

And soon, Confolens was back, telling him that the instructions had been carried out. He said, frowning: 'What's on your mind, Paul?'

'Just being careful. How far away is he?'

Confolens was peering over his shoulder at the outboard. 'Oh, five hundred and fifty yards, I'd say. If you want it precisely, there's a range-finder on the bridge.'

'No, it doesn't matter, five hundred yards isn't much for a good underwater swimmer. But we can afford a moment or two to make sure, I'd say. Wouldn't you?'

'Oh.'

'Yes indeed.'

He waited. Then: 'How fast is our dinghy?'

Confolens said: 'A Boston whaler-type, two hundred horse-power outboard. Say thirty-five knots if we have to push it.'

'You put guns on board?'

'Five rifles.'

'That's all we'll ever need. And there he is now.'

He passed the glass over to Confolens, and Confolens took them and stared out at the swimmer who was heading back to the boat, moving easily and swiftly through the water, keeping the feet well down, the arms at the breast stroke, not churning up any water, making no sign of an alien presence; there was just the head bobbing above the water, and as he watched, it went down again, out of his sight.

He said: 'My God, you're right, a frogman. We'd better move.'

'Just give me one more minute,' Paul said, 'you know this sector better than I do. Get a good look at him as he comes aboard. Tell me if we know him.'

Confolens held his stare. In a moment he said: 'Yes, we know him. Only it's a woman. Her name is Maria Consuelo Santiago, and she's – she was – General Faleira's new aide-de-camp, replacing Captain da Costa.'

Paul took the glasses quickly. 'Into the boat, then, fast. I'll follow.' He took one last look, and saw the woman climbing up into the boat, a lithe, slim, athletic young body, the water shining on the black bikini, her face covered by a mask, a small tube of oxygen strapped to her slender waist.

He saw her look back at the yacht, just once, and then she was signalling to the helmsman with a certain urgency; it looked as though she were telling him to get the hell out of there, fast. He saw the helmsman whom Confolens had known as the pineapple seller swing the tiller over, and then he was racing up the companionway after Confolens, leaping over the rail and landing in the water close by the dinghy.

He climbed aboard; the motor was already idling, and Manuel, grinning, threw open the throttle and let it surge into life. As Paul fell into the scuppers, he said:

'Straight out to sea. And we don't head back till the sun's gone down. Keep moving.'

The little dinghy shot forward, heading for the horizon at maximum throttle. Manuel was keeping the yacht between them and the outboard motorboat, and two men were lying in the stern with their rifles ready. There was a look of terror on Estrella's face, and Paul took her hand and said gently:

'There is nothing to worry about, nothing at all. I won't let them harm you if I have to stay with you night and day. Day . . . and night.'

And then, behind them, the yacht blew up.

There was a single massive explosion that ripped the hull in two and sent scattered debris of timber and steel plating flying through the air. The stern went down, and a finger of flame was coming up over the forepart. It nosed itself into the air as though seeking one more gasp of life; and then, with a massive rumble that came in shuddering waves to them across the water, it stood on its broken tail and slid backwards down into the depths of the ocean.

Of the outboard, at first, there was no sign; and then, with the high-powered glasses, they could just pick out the speck of it far away near the beach.

Paul said: 'Give us another three or four miles, cut the motors, and we'll sweat it out till dark.' He saw that Estrella had taken his hand in hers and was nervously rubbing it. He looked at Confolens and said: 'The radio?'

Confolens nodded: 'Short-wave, under the seat.'

'Can you reach Bramble?'

'Yes, I can.'

'Okay. Tell him to pick us up at the *Ponta do Arpoador*, thirty minutes after the sun goes down.'

Confolens pulled out the radio, and started tapping out his call-signal.

Paul lay back in the bottom of the boat, his head close to Estrella's thigh, and closed his eyes. And in two minutes he was fast asleep.

CHAPTER EIGHT

LARANJEIROS.
Co-ordinates: *22.51S:* *43.18W.*

A long, hard, haul up the steep mountainside from the ratchet-railway line at Laranjeiros, under the huge green acacias, the myrtles, rubber-trees, wild figs, and laurels, the broken road branched sharply into the forest.

Here, the last heavy rains had washed away the tarmac surface, so that the road itself hung like a thin ribbon of asphalt, only half of it left and the remainder of it down in the deep gorge; a man could walk with care along its inner flank, provided he kept his eyes off the great chasm beneath him and did not falter.

There were two hundred feet of this broken road, and in parts it was only two feet wide, and when he had crossed over, and was once more in the safety of the dark woods, Rick Meyers breathed a sigh of relief.

He found the freshly-cut scar on the casuarina tree that was the beginning of the marked trail, and followed the blaze-cuts for a little over a mile; he could see the cabin there, could smell the wood-smoke coming from its stone chimney, and he sat down on his haunches in the darkness and stared at it, looking for any sign of life. A candle was burning in one of the upper windows, and when his eyes got used to its pale glow, he could see a shadow moving on the wall behind it, gaunt and elongated. He cupped his hands around his mouth and whistled into them; it could have been the cry of a night-bird, a parakeet, perhaps, searching out the insects it fed on.

He waited.

In a little while, he heard a rustle near the door, and a match flared, and it was Braga.

He got to his feet and walked across the clearing where the beans were growing, and the stunted banana tree with the stream beside it. A cloud that was over the moon passed on, and in the momentary light he saw that the windows near the door were covered with heavy sacking. He put out his hand and took

Braga's, and they went inside together.

As Braga closed the door and locked it, the faint lights flared, and he saw a young woman there, part Indian and part Portuguese, a girl of eighteen or so, very slim and attractive, but with the bowed legs of the up-country women who were carrying loads on their backs as soon as they could walk. They never learned to crawl, he was thinking . . .

The girl smiled at him, and said: '*Boa noite, Senhor, seja bem-vindo*, you are welcome here.' It surprised him, and Braga smiled and said: 'My wife.' He used the word *mulher*, which could have meant *my woman*. 'And she speaks no English, none at all.'

'You are sure of that?'

The girl was still trimming the oil lamps, the yellow light gleaming on her smooth brown skin.

Braga shrugged: 'Yes, I am sure, she is family. My grandfather came here from Portugal, many years ago, as you know, and this girl . . . the daughter of my second cousin's first wife, from the Ruachi country up on the River, an Indian girl really, with just enough foreign blood to make her at least semi-civilised.' The white of his teeth was gleaming in the pale light, and there was sweat on his face. He said: 'But if anyone should come this way, if anyone should wonder, she is my woman. She knows what I am doing, and she can be trusted. Even the second cousin of a second cousin . . . for the Ruachi Indians, it's family, and not to be betrayed.'

The young girl had found a bottle of *pinga* in the plank cupboard, and was pouring it into two glasses for them, and when she had finished she stood at the kitchen door and said: '*Esta pronto, se gostaria do almocar* . . . ' Braga looked at Rick and said: 'Hungry? You must be, she's a good cook.'

He nodded to her, and when she had gone out, Braga leaned back on the rickety wooden chair, its seat of woven cord, and said: 'It's good to see you, Rick, to feel among friends again. It's been a nightmare. Every time a new man turns up, they subject him to such a scrutiny . . . it makes we wonder how I ever got in among them, wonder if they're on to me, have been all the time and are just stringing me along.'

'No,' Rick said, 'they're not on to you. You've learned too much about them. If they'd suspected you, you'd have learned nothing except what it feels like to be dead.' He looked around the tiny cabin, the bare plank walls, the adze-cut furniture. 'What is this place?'

Braga grinned. His boyish face was dimpled like a girl's, and his eyes were sparkling. He said: 'This place is my house, my hideout, I'm buying it from the owner with two days' work a week on his bean crop for the next three seasons. It's hard work to keep the jungle at bay.' His grin widened. 'And we had a meeting here last evening. That's what they do, a different hideout each time. It means I've been promoted, it also means they checked up on my background and found it stood up.'

'I should hope so.'

Meyers had spent a week on nothing else, fabricating a past for a known and dangerous terrorist from the savage hill country of the Serra Negra, with half the police of Maranhao searching for him, a young outlaw named Jorge Braga, with seven murders to his credit and a lifetime in prison hanging over his head. Not even the police knew that the man they were hunting for was a soldier of fortune from Portugal who had spent only five of his thirty-two years in Brazil; and that with Confolens.

Myers let him talk. He knew the strain he'd been under these past weeks, knew the need to relax, to feel safe . . . Braga stretched his limbs luxuriously and said:

'Santarem has taken over the Xirista army in the north. He is the number two man, next to Juan Xira himself, and perhaps he's more dangerous than any of them. Xira calculates the dangers he's facing, very carefully, and won't go in till the odds are about even. But Santarem . . . he's a madman. His idea of relaxation is to go up to a squad of police, and say, "My name is Santarem, you're looking for me,' and then pull out his gun and start shooting. Xira doesn't really trust him too much. But then, he doesn't trust anybody. Anyway . . . ' He sipped his *pinga*, and said: 'We'll have some food soon, *Feijao*, of course, but it wouldn't be wise to start eating steaks.' He said gloomily: 'Beans, day after day, but she cooks them well, with a guava paste, you've eaten *goiabada*? And she caught a partridge this morning, so it won't be too bad.'

Meyers waited.

Braga refilled their glasses, and sat down again, and said at last: 'And aren't you going to ask why I called you here?'

'I am a patient man,' Meyers said. 'When you're ready.' He could see the excitement in Braga's eyes.

'They were all here, a meeting, all except Xira. Santarem, on his way north, with Juliao, Ajuda and Arrifana. For a while I was tempted, a well thrown hand grenade would have solved a lot of problems, but . . . we'd still have Xira on the loose, and so I held back. Was I right?'

Meyers was nodding: 'You were right.'

'And Arrifana . . . are you ready for this? I got a good look at him, checked it out with the photographs. Arrifana is Brigadier da Sao Andres Lorenzo. That explains a lot, doesn't it? I don't know how long he's been a Xirista, but a man from the Defense Ministry in their ranks? It's incredible! Juliao is the bomb expert, he can make a powerful explosive out of rotten eggs . . . '

Meyers murmured: 'Sulphuretted hydrogen, even that's possible, in theory . . . '

'. . . and Ajuda is in charge of the sabotage squads. I've prepared a list, on tape, of forty-eight sites that have already been prepared for demolition, the Presidential Palace and the Parliament building included, as well as a dozen others we didn't know about. The American Embassy is not to be destroyed after all; Xira has passed the word that the blame is to be put on the C.I.A., and he figured that it would be going too far if they assassinated their own Ambassador. But there is one interesting addition to the list. Did you know that the Bolivian exiles have an office in Rio?'

'I know it. On Rua Paula Freitas, the Brazilian police have been keeping an eye on it for a long time now. And so have we.'

'Not long enough. Apparently, that was mined two months ago, and the reason they're blowing it sky high . . . the Bolivian general, what's his name?'

'Ramon Huachi.'

'Yes, General Huachi and all his top lieutenants are having a meeting to decide just how much more they can afford to support Juan Xira, how far they can let him get before they move in and seize the border provinces. Xira's got a pretty good intelligence outfit of his own, the names that were flying around the table this evening . . . '

'And I hope your tape-recorder hasn't been giving you trouble?' Meyers said mildly.

Braga beamed: 'One hour and seven minutes of it. It's all ready for you. Anyway . . . *Pinga?*'

Was he drinking too much? There was no slurring to his speech, no more than the usual brightness to his eyes. Meyers passed over his glass in silence, and Braga filled it again for him; it was harsh and rough on his throat, and he wished he had some of Colonel Tobin's Irish.

Braga said: 'Anyway . . . Xira found out about this meeting, and deduced – probably rightly – that the Bolivians would hit him the moment he began to seize power, as soon as he'd taken

88

over the radio stations and broadcast news of the government's overthrow. So he is hitting them first, and hard, at the same time that he hits the government. They'll all be together, including General Ramon Huachi, and by shoving his grimy thumb on a few buttons . . . poof! Exit the Bolivian threat. Exit the Brazilian government. And enter . . . Juan Xira. The Xira era.' He said again, savoring the words, enjoying himself: 'The Xira era of applied and carefully calculated terrorism. At eleven o'clock exactly, on Wednesday night, he'll push the buttons that blow up the Parliament, the four main army barracks, the three electrical plants, the radio stations he doesn't want to use, and the offices of thirty-one people he wants out of his way before he makes his announcement. In his speech, he's declaring a State of Emergency, and he's carefully keeping to the old Constitution, which means that under the emergency he has full powers as Dictator – arrest without warrant, imprisonment without trial, capital punishment back on the statutes, and the revocation of all civil rights. No appeal against the decisions of his military tribunals, and . . . you know who is handling the tribunals? Alacrimo, ex-Colonel of the Brazilian artillery, fired for corruption, imprisoned for bribing the jurors at his trial, and still holding out about that large bank account in Buenos Aires.'

'And at a guess,' Meyers said, 'once Alacrimo has applied his very considerable know how to the new cause, once all of Xira's enemies, real or potential, have been executed, it's a distinct possibility that Alacrimo himself will be the next to face a firing squad.'

'Or,' Braga said dryly, 'to lead the *next* revolution.'

The young Indian girl was there at the kitchen door, a tray in her hands, the food steaming. The smell of the *feijao* was rich and ripe. She said, smiling: *'Com permissao? May I?'*

She came in and placed the steaming plates of beans, and partridge, and the *goiabada*, on the table, and gave them forks to eat with, instead of their fingers, out of deference to the foreign guest, and then she went and sat in a corner and waited for them to eat.

She sat there demurely on a wooden stool, her bare ankles turned in, her long, delicately-fingered hands in her lap; they all had those beautiful hands, the Indian women, mobile and expressive; you could tell their life's history by watching the easy movements of the fingers, the subtle articulation of the wrists. Her eyes were cast down, correctly, not watching them at their food.

Meyers smiled, and he said gently: 'If I were not here, she would be eating with you.'

'All right. If you are sure you wouldn't take offense.' Braga was laughing quietly, playing his role as an up-country Indian and enjoying it. He turned to the girl and said: 'Our guest would be honored if you would sit with us.'

It was a family joke between them that he used the conventional, the over-polite 'A senhora', and she giggled to hide her embarrassment, a hand over her white teeth, and then she went to the kitchen and came back with her own plate, a correctly minimal portion, and sat down hesitantly with them.

Her huge dark eyes were on Meyers constantly as they ate, and when she had cleared away the dishes, and had taken her seat there again, and was pouring him his sixth glass of *pinga*, he heard her say something, very low, in an Indian dialect he had never even heard before.

Was it mischief that was in those eyes now? Something was amusing her, deeply. He saw Braga look at her momentarily – but only momentarily – startled. And then he was smiling again, very pleased with the way things were going, looking down at his glass and toying with his drink, as though he were making up his mind whether to translate or not.

He said at last: 'She is a Ruachi, mostly. Do you know the Ruachi Indians?'

'No,' Meyers shook his head. 'I know roughly where they come from, nothing about them at all. They are obviously very handsome people.'

They were talking Portuguese now, and Meyers was only dimly aware that the language had been changed, that Braga himself had changed it.

He said again: 'No, I don't know very much about them, I'm afraid.'

'Then you must ask Confolens, he knows them well.'

'Confolens knows everything well.'

'Yes, he does.' He said, smiling very faintly: 'It's hard to move in and out of my cover so smoothly. With you, I'm a Portuguese, from Lisbon, the most civilised city in the world, and the most beautiful. With her . . . ' He broke off. 'She is family, a cousin, I don't sleep with her, did I tell you that?'

'Yes, I gathered.'

The heat in the tiny cabin was stifling; the peppers she'd ground into the *goiabada* were causing rivulets of sweat to run down his back, over his face, down his chest.

Braga said, and he was beaming now, delighted with his own thoughts, delighted with the chance to talk freely:

'A civilised Portuguese, having dinner with a friend from . . . who knows from where? But with her, I'm an Indian, just like the rest of them, with a plate of *feijao* and a bottle of *pinga*, and it doesn't help at all that there's a touch of the European in my blood somewhere, or that I'm eating with a fork instead of with my fingers. I'm an Indian, back inside my cover, and that's the way it should be. Even with you, I should never forget I am an Indian. But we'll have coffee, nonetheless. Hot, and black, and sweet, and as strong as you've ever drunk in your life. If Brazil had given nothing else to civilisation, she'd always be remembered for her coffee.'

He turned to the girl: '*O cafe, por favor.*' Even the *please* was the *por favor* of the Brazilians, instead of his natural *faca favor*.

The young woman looked at Rick and smiled, and it was much, much more than the smile of a hostess for her guest. She went to the kitchen, and in moment he heard her grinding the coffee-beans, smelled the ripe scent of them as she pulverised them in the mortar. He fingered his glass, a cut-down beer bottle, wondering if he could crush it in his hand, and he said at last, knowing that Braga had a secret, a good one, up his sleeve:

'You were telling me about the Ruachi Indians, Jorge.'

'Ah yes, I was . . . moving in and out of my cover all the time, and now I'm a Ruachi again, one of those savage, but charmingly unsophisticated Indians, and the manners in my tribe are legendary. Cruder, perhaps, than the manners of the Portuguese, but more basic, more down to earth, more . . . ' He broke off, the smile still playing over his dark face. He said dreamily: 'My grandfather came here from Portugal, and one day, maybe, I will go back there and see the country he came from.' He was openly laughing now, enjoying his secret joke. And stalling too, Meyers was thinking. Waiting for the girl, perhaps?

She came at last with the coffee, and poured it and sat down again with them, and looked at Braga expectantly.

Braga said: 'Among the Ruachi, Rick, when a stranger comes to a man's house in the night, he sleeps with the man's woman. It's the customary thing to do. And my cousin reminded me of my duties. She wants you to sleep with her tonight.'

Meyers wished he'd spoken in English. But he hadn't; the language was Portuguese, and the girl was looking at him expectantly, not embarrassed, not inquisitive, not shy . . . merely waiting for his answer, the expectant look of the grand duchess who has said: 'And would you care for another cup of coffee, Mr Meyers?'

He glanced at Braga, and Braga said gently: 'I told you, Rick, she's not my mistress. Family. And I'm out of my cover again. But even back in it . . . '

He had told Bramble: *'I've got to get some sleep, I'll get Braga to put me up for what's left of the night, I'll see you some time in the morning . . . '*

He looked at the girl: *'Qual e o seu nome?* What is your name?' *'Chamo-me Suele.'*

Suele, all that was left of Consuelo after they'd finished with it . . .

'Suele. *Chamo-me Rick.'*

'Rick. *Gosto muito,* I like it.'

'E muito linda, you are very beautiful.'

'E voce e muito simpatico.'

He looked at Braga. He said. 'You're Portuguese, Jorge.'

'But she's is an Indian. And you have the opportunity, now, to hurt her beyond any measure you can imagine.'

'You are sure of that?'

'I'm sure of it.' They had switched to English again. 'We are Indians, both of us.'

He waited while she washed the dishes, and he drank three more glasses of *pinga,* knowing that he too could slip out of his expertise tonight and be a human being once again, and when she was finished, she came in and took his hand and smiled at him, and led him into the bedroom, and slept with him on top of the bed, naked and desirable in the steaming night, her smooth brown skin like polished amber, her cool flesh hard and resilient under his probing hands.

And, in the morning, when the sun was still low and filtering its light through the trees, she brought him his coffee and knelt beside him while he drank it, running her long fingers over his chest and resting her head on his thigh, and then he found Braga and took the tape from him, and set off once more across the dangerous, broken road that would take him back to the town.

CHAPTER NINE

CORRAL DAS PEDRAS.
Co-ordinates: 04.31S   54.01W.

The Xirista army was on the move.

They had come from the Illha de Marajo at the Delta of the Amazon's vast watershed; from the rugged highlands off the Morro Grosso; from the unknown hinterland of Bareto; and from the thousands of riverside villages that dotted the Amazon's widely-separated banks.

And they had come to fight.

Not because they thought that fighting would improve their condition; they were far too sophisticated to believe that. It was because fighting, for all of them, had been a constant way of life for as far back as they could remember. They fought the army, and the police, and among themselves – and most of all they fought the Indian tribes who had nothing to be killed for, whose empty existence should, perhaps, have been a sort of protection in itself. Why should a man be killed when his death can profit nobody?

But for the *mestizos* there was always a profit, and the profit was the blood-lust itself. A man would be slaughtered for the cheap beads he carried, for a yard-long strip of bark-cloth, or for his pathetically inefficient spear. For years now, the Indians had been driven to work for the *mestizos*, tapping the wild rubber that grew in the jungle. And the wild tappers, the *borracheros* as they called themselves, were universally feared and hated.

The *borracheros* would descend on the villages at night – they could move like Indians in the darkness of the jungle they knew so well – and would round up every man, woman and child, and take them out into the forests in their constant search for the latex that brought them their profits.

The pattern was always the same; the village would be surrounded, a few shots would be fired, and then two or three of the chiefs would be tied to the nearest trees and simply flogged until they were dead, a lesson to all the others. And then, they would be taken out and put to work, and of every twenty, six or seven died, from overwork or malnutrition, and the *borracheros* would send the wicker-baskets of rubber-sap down to others of their kind in the river-towns, and other Indians would boil the juice and reduce it to its proper consistency. The women would do this work, and the mortality rate was very high among them, too, though they usually died from the excesses of their masters. And once more, it would be sent on its way to the coast, and the *borracheros* would line their pockets with the money.

But now the price of raw wild rubber was dropping, had been dropping for many years, and the tappers were driven back to something they really preferred – outright banditry. They would ride into the towns on their ponies, and rob, rape, murder as they pleased; there was no law in the river villages, no law at all. And where there was, perhaps, a solitary guard put there by a hopeful government that knew it could never control the excesses of the outlaws, or a small post of the Military – these unfortunates would be the first to die. And they would not die easily, either; hatred was as much a part of the *borracheros*' life as was the fighting itself.

But now, a quietly savage man had come from the south, and had told them – it seemed incredible to them – that he was forming a new government, that all the vast acreage of the Indians which the Bureau of Indian Affairs had been working on their behalf, would be handed to them, the wild rubber tappers, to do with as they pleased. He had told them there would be amnesty for them; and not only amnesty but revenge, because he wanted every man who ever wore a uniform out of his way. He told them the National Treasury would be looted, and that the money would be shared among them, more *cruzeiros* than they could count, and gold, too, for the asking . . .

And he told them that they needed, for a while, the Indians themselves. For cannon-fodder, he said. He had said: 'The government and the Indians, they are our enemies. Let them kill each other off. And then we will control the country, to run it as we see fit.'

The quietly savage man was Juan Xira. He needed the *mestizos*, the huge hordes of *borracheros*, for his own purposes. He needed them to destroy the army that was his enemy. And when they had served his purpose, no doubt he would find a way to get rid of them too.

*

Miguel Sampaio was whispering to himself the words of the prayer his grandmother had taught him twenty-three years ago in the lovely old house in Belem.

The ropes were cutting into his wrists, pulling his arms out as he hung there, and his naked back was raw and bloodied from the lash. The blood was running down his thighs and into his boots, and when he moved his toes it squelched, as though he had been wading through the swamps and had filled them with the wet slimy mud of the marshes. He wondered, almost hysterically, if his boots could fill up and overflow and if, by then, there would be any more blood left in his broken body.

The *mestizo* was squatting on a log in front of him, cleaning his teeth with a piece of frayed stick, and grinning at him stupidly. He said: 'Now tell me, Sampaio, tell me that you are a government spy, I don't want to flog you to death for nothing. Tell me.'

The lash did not stop falling across his shoulders, and the pain of it was unbearable. Sampaio said, gritting his teeth: 'You are mad! My name is Miguel Sampaio, I am a gem-cutter from Sao Paulo.' The end of the lash flicked around his belly, and opened up a four-inch gash. He tried hard not to scream, and he shouted: 'If you kill me, you kill one of your best men! You are mad!'

He had not seen the signal, but the whipping stopped, and the *mestizo* got up from the trunk he had been sitting on and came close to him and said: 'I could drive a knife into your stomach now, spy. Perhaps I will do that in the morning if you are still alive. Or the morning after, or the morning after that.'

Miguel's eyes were closed, his chin on his chest. He felt the *mestizo* thumb back and eyelid, the callouses bearing hard on the eyeball. What was his name? Jugasto? A big, swarthy man who commanded four hundred of the Indians, and had nothing but contempt for them. He saw the evil, grinning face, peering into his, and then a hand was over his heart, feeling its beat, and Jugasto said: 'Twenty, thirty more, he can stand it. Then leave him there. Stand guard on him.'

He kept his eyes open now as the lash came down again, and watched Jugasto walk away, down the narrow track that led to the clearing where the others were camped. He looked at the *mestizo* who was whipping him, and said, gasping his pain: 'Do you . . . do you believe . . . I am a spy?'

The whipping did not stop, nor lose its force.

His name was Xantara, a giant of a man with a thick red

95

beard. 'No, I do not believe it. But I've got my orders, Miguel. Fifteen more, just hang on. Maybe tomorrow you'll convince him, who knows?' He went on whipping, sweat running down his face, and said: 'Who even cares? Twelve . . . ten . . . eight, seven, six . . .'

Five more? The haze over his eyes was thickening, and there was only bright blue on his horizon, with sudden, startling lights that went on and off rapidly, changing from blue to red, the red of his own blood. And then, it was all black, and he hung there, his feet just clear of the ground, and the last thing he heard before he lost consciousness and the coma came over him, was a strangled gasp and the heavy sound of Xantara's great body falling.

He did not hear Hanson's voice, or feel the hands that groped for him and cut him down, did not feel himself being carried at a fast, incredibly fast, trot along the winding jaguar-trail that led deep and ever deeper into the jungle.

Hanson held him in his arms like a baby, running, bending low where the vines were a groping tangle around his head, and he did not slow down till he had covered more than a mile and had come to the edge of the river, one of the thousands of unnamed rivers that, sooner or later, would find their way into the giant Amazon itself.

He laid Sampaio down on the moss at the water's edge, on his stomach, and slit the laces of the jungle boots and pulled them off, and winced when he saw the blood that poured out of them. He emptied the pack of sulphanilamide powder from his first-aid kit and poured it all over the pulp of his back, and dusted it in and took off his own shirt to cover it, and then took out the flask, and rolled him over, and poured some of the staff Irish down his throat.

Sampaio's eyes flickered. And when they opened fully, he looked up at Hanson and said, gasping: 'You sonofabitch, where were you?'

Hanson's own face was filled with the vicarious pain. He said: 'I was there, watching, all the time. Wasn't much I could do till one of them moved out, their campsite was only a hundred feet away.'

'Yes, yes, I know.' He rolled his eyes and said: 'Sonofabitch. You know they killed Heinnemann?'

'We know. Edgars got out.'

'Ah yes, Edgars, never thought he'd make it. Now I'm out too, by the looks of it.'

'All to the good.' Hanson grinned. 'The balloon's about to go up, we'd have had to pull you out anyway.' Sampaio groaned and tried to roll over, and Hanson helped him sit up and said: 'Are you going to live, do you think? That's a damn fool question, isn't it? You'll live.'

'That bastard Jugasto. If I ever get my hands on him . . . Xantara too . . .'

'Xantara?'

'A nobody. The man who was beating me, doing what he was told. Poor sonofabitch, no authority at all.' He looked at Hanson and said: 'But he's dead, isn't he? I heard you . . . I heard you hit him before I blacked out.'

'Yes, he's dead enough for all intents and purposes, couldn't be much deader if he tried. Only question is, what am I going to do with you now? Carry you back, help you walk, or whistle up a stretcher?'

He took off his helmet and eased the micro-miniature radio there, and slipped it on again, the tiny mike at his throat, and said: 'Jaguar? Come in, Jaguar. This is ground-hog.'

He looked at Sampaio and grinned; 'Ground-hog, why did they have to call me that?'

He was still panting after his long-hard run. He took a swig of the whiskey himself, and when Jaguar answered, he said: 'I've got him. He's okay. Well, not exactly okay, he's pretty mad at everybody, me included. What? Hell, I don't know what he's supposed to have, nobody tells me anything.' He listened for a while, and glared at Sampaio and said: 'You're supposed to know where they're headed, and if you don't, I'm going to throw you right back to them till you find out.'

Sampaio nodded, and Hanson said: 'Send someone out to meet us, to give me a hand with him, can you do that? We'll start on in now, along the same route, look for the nice marks I've made on the trees. Okay, over and out.'

He took off his helmet again and tossed it down, and scooped up some water from the river and threw it over his face, and turned to Sampaio and said: 'Anything I can do to make you more comfortable?'

'Nada.'

'Think you can walk?'

'Give me my boots, we'll find out.'

'They're full of blood.'

Hanson washed them out in the river, and said: 'They want to know if you got the information you're supposed to have.

You'd better let me have it, in case you drop dead on the way back.'

Sampaio began to cough horribly, retching blood, and he said: 'Sonofabitch, he broke one of my ribs. Yes, I got it. They're massing at Itapixuna, on the eastern bank, seven miles above its junction with the Xingu. Give me some more of that whiskey, will you?' Hanson handed him the flask. He said dryly: 'Best thing in the world for a punctured lung, I bet the medics don't even know that.'

'The hell with the medics.' Sampaio drank deeply, and coughed again, and there were tears in his eyes. He said carefully: 'The *mestizos* are all together there, seven thousand of them, and it seems to me that they're pretty heavily armed. Machine-guns, mortars, fourteen pieces of heavy artillery, twenty-eight pieces of light.' His voice was very weak. 'The idea is . . . they're going to entice the Brazilian army out, fall back through the Indians, let the Indians and the army fight it out, then move in and mop up what's left on both sides.'

Hanson said: 'How many Indians? That's the crucial question, isn't it?'

'Are you ready for this? Fifty-two thousand of them. They've only got rifles, and their poisoned arrows, but even so . . . sheer numbers alone, they're going to make one hell of a dent in the army. They'll prance around on the outskirts of them, in and out of the jungle . . . you know how they fight.'

Hanson said: 'Ha! The Colonel's had the Brazilian army withdrawn, they won't be there. But we will.'

Sampaio stared: 'We're not going to fight those poor sonofabitch Indians, I hope? A hundred of us? Against fifty thousand of them?'

'No,' Hanson shook his head, 'we tangle with the *mestizos*, the real headache. Once we get rid of them, the Indians will fold their tents and steal silently off in the night, just like it says in the books. We don't have any quarrel with them, the poor bastards. We'll just keep out of their way, all the same, I don't fancy a poisoned arrow up my arse. You feel like making a move?'

'Any time you say.'

'Anything else you have to report?'

'That's about the size of it.' Sampaio said again: 'The east bank . . . of the Itapixuna . . . seven miles up from the junction.'

'I've got it. Your boots.'

Sampaio slipped his boots back on, his movements laboured and painful. He climbed to his feet and would have fallen if

Hanson had not put out an arm to steady him, and together they moved off slowly along the riverbank, then found the place where the blazed trail began, and cut deeply into the forest.

It was dark now, the darkness coming on them suddenly, but Hanson moved steadily onwards, leading the way, checking the yellow cuts on the tree-trunks as he passed them.

Once, he said, branching off: 'This way, we can make a short cut here . . . ' and they came back on to the trail again fifteen minutes later. Across a wide clearing of pampas grass, a solitary casuarina standing tall and majestic in its center, a sentinel in the moonlight, and he grinned and said: 'Another hour, how are you holding up? Okay?'

Sampaio was coughing again: 'Okay. I'm making too much goddam noise.'

'Don't worry about it. Back into the forest for a couple of miles, and we'll hit the first of the outposts.'

But three men were coming towards them, runnning easily through the long grass, and Hanson's rifle was ready; Sampaio heard the soft click of the safety-catch, and he said: 'It's Ramatul Singh, two others.' His eyes were marvellous in the darkness.

The Sikh always wore his turban, even in the field, and his black beard was bristling fiercely. The two men with him were the medics, Jason and Chiffick, and they were lugging a stretcher with them, the base-issue field packs slung over their shoulders.

Ramatul Singh said briskly: 'All right, this is where you both take a rest, give me please your flashlights, you two, sit down please, under the tree, if you will.'

Hanson said patiently: 'We're nearly there, Singh, let's just make it back as soon as we can, shall we?'

The Sikh looked at him, his black eyes bright: 'And who are you to give me orders, it's the other man who is hurt. Ah, I see you have blood on your lips, it is blue blood, isn't it?'

Sampaio said: 'I'm a natural-born aristocrat, you bearded bastard.' But he sat down and let the Sikh look at him, and when the Indian gently pulled away the shirt that was sticking to him, he gasped with the pain and watched the men break out the wide bandages, and Hanson said:

'I'm going on, I'll leave him with you.' The information Sampaio had given him was burned into his brain; it even pained him.

The Sikh nodded: 'We'll run back with him when we are finished, we'll be there before you, isn't it? Isn't it?'

'Okay.' Hanson squatted down on his haunches in front of

Sampaio. He said: 'You want to be a Sergeant, Miguel? Boss all the boys around, give 'em hell once in a while? Because, if you want it or not, I'm going to have a word with Paul.'

Sampaio was grinning. He said: 'A staff whiskey before you go. If I'm a sergeant, I'm entitled to it.'

'Oh no,' Sikh said. 'Blue blood, a lung in very bad trouble, please, no whiskey.'

Hanson passed over the flask and watched Sampaio drink happily, and screwed on the top again and set off through the tall pampas grass, running lightly, knowing that soon the captain would be listening to all he had to say.

He kept saying to himself over and over, as he ran: 'By Christ, they stripped his back clear down to the bone.'

He wondered if the captain had got back yet from his hunting trip up the river, with Blackman, the expert; next to Confolens, Blackman was the country's foremost authority on the Amazon tribes, a civilian, really, but as ready for a fight as the best of them. He said to himself moodily: 'I'll bet he got back with a couple of prisoners, I'll bet he already knows all about Itapixuna . . . that poor bastard Sampaio, right down to the bare bones. And for what?'

He ran on, fast.

Captain Duyvel had a drunken Indian on his hands when Hanson came in, and two others who were not yet drunk but getting there fast.

One of them, plump and effeminate-looking, and so drunk he could hardly stand, was a man, very short and stubby, with bulging muscles and almost nothing to cover his nakedness. He wore a string round his waist, to which was attached a leather bag that served both as a cod-piece and a pocket; in it, he carried all his worldly possessions – a crab-shell, carried by some unknown hand from the distant sea, in which to strain the arrow-poison he would make every new moon from the boiled roots of the *strychnos* tree, three spare arrow-heads made from old and rusted bolts which he heated over a charcoal fire and hammered into shape, honing them to a marvellous sharpness afterward on a flat piece of granite, and a hunk of flintstone which he would use to make fire whenever he needed it, which was not very often.

The other two were his women, and they were both stark naked except for the blankets which Duyvel had given them to cover themselves with, and which they merely wore loosely over their heads as they sat on the grass, like tents, reaching out from time to time for the *pinga* bottle which their man was hogging.

One of the women was his wife, some thirty or thirty-five years old (it was very hard to tell with the Sasanico Indians; their women, at thirty, were already old crones). And the other, a skinny thing of twelve or thirteen years, was his favorite daughter.

There was a line of deep scratches down Duyvel's face, and he looked at Hanson and grinned, jerking his head at the young girl.

He said: 'Don't get too close, for Christ's sake. I put a blanket over her shoulders, and she thought, hell, she thought I was trying to rape her, look what she did to my face. What have you got?'

Hanson said, panting, squatting down on his heels like an Indian himself: 'Plenty. Is it safe to talk?'

'Hell yes, they don't speak any known language at all. Animals. But kinda cute. The only word he knows . . . ' he jerked a thumb at the man, 'is *pinga*. Brandy. All he knows. And man, can he put it away. We're on the fourth bottle.'

Blackman was there with him, his jungle clothes covered with the slime of the rivers, a sparse, angular man in his early fifties. He said, sighing: 'We're going to have to get Confolens up here, the only man who might really understand what he's talking about.'

Blackman had written a learned treatise on the languages of the Amazon, and Colonel Tobin had hired him, at more money in a month than he made in a year at the London University, specifically for this enterprise.

He said pathetically: 'I can speak eighteen Indian dialects, can you believe that? *Eighteen!* Fluently. I could translate Dante's Inferno into ten or twelve of them, but these people . . . whoever heard of the Sasanicos?' He said soberly: 'I have, that's who. The Sasanicos were the people who gave the Amazon its name, did you know that?'

Not waiting for anyone to answer him, he said: 'Francisco de Orellana, the man who first discovered the Amazon, he tried to cover its whole length, one of Pizarro's men . . . but he deserted, and when he got back to Europe he told the world that in the marvellous new watershed he had discovered, he was constantly attacked by warrior Indian women. And so, it got to be called the Amazon.'

He snorted. 'We're on the wrong side of the Atlantic, did you know that? The called the Indians Indians because they thought they've discovered India, and they called the Amazon the Amazon because they thought those warriors were women. But they weren't. They were just fat, pudgy, and terribly dangerous Sasanicos. Their men look like women, only if you get close enough to make sure . . . you get to be eaten, isn't that nice? The greatest Indian fighters in the world. Well, let's try again.' He said: 'My God, maybe I'd better have some more of that *pinga* myself.'

Hanson was looking at the young girl. No one could have called her beautiful; her nose was squat, her cheekbones too high, and there were tattoo-marks all over her face, over her tiny pointed breasts, and down her thighs; there was a porcupine quill through her nose too. But there was a certain animal grace in the way she moved, not like a woman at all, but more like a cat, on her hands and knees, crawling towards her father and reaching for the bottle and then withdrawing on to her haunches when he refused to give it to her. Her head moved quickly from side to side, taking in everything that was around her, accepting it.

Hanson said cheerfully: 'You realise you could buy that for six feet of bark-cloth? Think of the marvellous time you could have.'

Blackman said: 'Six feet of bark-cloth, or two rusted bolts for arrow-heads, or a dime store pocket-knife, or an empty beer bottle. No,' he corrected himself, 'for an empty beer bottle, you'd get his wife as well, and then . . . God help you. But if you're interested in animal behaviour, watch his eyes. He knows what a rifle is. It's my guess he knows how to use it. Well, back to purgatory.'

He squatted down again and began to talk, very softly and slowly, with the Indian.

Captain Duyvel looked at Hanson. 'What have you got?'

Hanson repeated all that Sampaio had told him, and added: 'And I'll bet that's what you're finding out from *them*.'

Duyvel shook his head: 'No, not quite. Let's look at the map.' He spread the map over the ground and studied it, and said at last: 'It checks nicely. Our drunken friend says the Indians have all been ordered into this area here, that's four miles east of the Itapixuna, all falling together nicely. Nothing I like better than corroboration, Intelligence is no good without it. It looks like the end of the road, doesn't it?'

'Provided they're ready in Rio.'

'Yes . . . Rio, a question of meshing the gears together, isn't it? Of all the balloons going pop at the same instant. Sampaio?'

'On his way in. Hurt badly, but in good hands now.' He looked

102

at the girl, at her little pot-belly, and said: 'I wonder when she had her last meal?'

'I gave her some roast peccary,' Duyvel said. 'She threw it at me, tried to beat the hell out of me again. So what are you going to do? But we've learned one thing. His tribe, with all its subdivisions, lives along the Paruari River. All the men, and some of the women too, have been armed with rifles and taken east. By water, overland, on foot and in trucks, on the water again . . . Ten *mestizos* with them. They have all been promised the one thing they ever dream about. Land.'

'Land. It's a little sad, isn't it? All the land in the world here, and all they want . . . is a little piece of it to call their own.'

'They've been told that if they kill enough of the soldiers, it will be parcelled out among them.'

Hanson said: 'You've got to hand it to those *mestizos*. How long does it take them to teach an Indian to use a rifle?'

Blackman stood up. He said: 'Half a day. They're taught to aim instinctively, the same way they aim a blow-pipe. They've been told that the government soldiers have guns too, but that their bullets will turn to water because they have offended the great god Sinca-Xulo. He doesn't know how many men there are in his tribe, because he can only count to ten, because that's their cycle-number, and anything beyond that is beyond their comprehension too. Like infinity for us, does that make you ponder a little? But he says they number ten times ten times ten, and you have to keep on repeating that until you fall asleep. His idea of infinity.' He sighed. 'Actually, the Sasanicos number about eight thousand, according to the only authoritative count we have – Confolens! But take it from me all of them are under arms and ready to die. For Juan Xira and his rabble of maniacs. And they've never even heard of him, or of the principle he stands for.'

Duyvel said, brooding: 'What happens when we let them go?'

Blackman shrugged: 'When we found them, they were stragglers, left behind in the great migration east. He'll either go back to his own piece of jungle, or . . . I don't know, maybe he'll decide he should be with the rest of his people. When he sobers up.'

'Uh-huh. So keep him talking. Milk him dry, and we'll turn him loose.'

Blackman squatted down again on his heels, and went on talking. He was having difficulty with the language, gesticulating, searching out suitable phrases. And suddenly . . . suddenly the

103

Indian lurched forward, throwing himself past Hanson and reaching out for the rifle which Hanson had propped against the tree. He worked the bolt with astonishing speed, and pointed it at Blackman, his tormentor, and pulled the trigger. When the hammer fell on an empty chamber, he looked at it in surprise, and then hurled it away, and squatted back on his haunches as though nothing untoward was happening.

Blackman said: 'My God . . . '

Hanson shrugged. 'You didn't think I'd leave a loaded rifle lying around, did you?' Mocking, he said: 'Somewhere around page eighty-two of the Manual, there's a whole paragraph on leaving loaded guns lying around. But I see what you mean.'

Duyvel said to Blackman: 'Tell him . . . tell him the bullets were turned to water. Tell him that's what will happen to *all* the Indians' rifles if they work for the *mestizos*.' He smiled, wondering if it would do any good, any good at all. He said gently: 'I don't suppose it will help, but if he convinces even one of his tribesmen . . . that's what military strategy is about, isn't it? Confusing the enemy?'

Blackman worked it all out and told him, and when he had finished, he said: '*Usu bri asaga hasi f'rinaga*, take the women and go now.'

The Indian looked at his wife, at his daughter, and back at Blackman. He nodded his head vigorously, which meant, in his language: *No*.

Blackman insisted: '*F'rinaga, f'rinaga, asaga hasi*, with the women, you go.'

The Indian went on nodding, violently, insisting: '*Ama wilina, kriku wilina, krikamisa wilina*.'

Blackman sighed. He said, translating: 'I belong to you, the woman belongs to you, the virgin belongs to you. They're all yours, Duyvel. Doesn't that make you a happy man? And do you mind if I go and get some sleep now?'

Captain Duyvel hesitated. He unslung the rifle that was over his shoulder, and said slowly: 'It's loaded, Academic interest, I want to know, so be ready.'

Blackman was smiling, nodding his head. 'Yes, it should be most interesting, go ahead.'

Duyvel held out the rifle in both his hands to the Indian, the symbolic offering; and the Indian took it from him in both his hands too, and held it for a moment, and then, just as symbolically passed it back again, nodding his head in the negative, and saying (very slowly and clearly because he knew the devil in the

104

bottle was tying his tongue into knots):

'*Kasaru . . . xlimarix . . . u saliso maniburi.*'

Blackman said sadly: 'It is for you . . . to take my life . . . because I am your slave.' He sighed. 'Your baby, Duyvel. I'm going to bed.'

He walked away from them, and Captain Duyvel turned and called after him:

'Wait! How far can I trust him now? Have you any idea at all?'

Blackman said: 'He'll lay down his life . . . he'll sacrifice both his women for you. You're his master now. Good night.'

He was gone, the darkness swallowing him up.

CHAPTER TEN

THE MATO GROSSO.
Co-ordinates: 12.28S. 57.20W.

Colonel Tobin had set up his headquarters in the Mato Grosso, at a point equidistant from the two spheres of operation, halfway between Rio and the turbulent waters of the Itapixuna River.

And to all who knew he was there, it could only mean one thing; the Private Army was ready to go into action. The ground-work had been done, the intelligence collated, the deductions drawn, the tactics planned. Now, it was up to Paul and Bramble; and the Colonel was poised above them, ready to see that his orders were obeyed, down to the last, last letter.

He said to Charles: 'The country's too damn big, our striking forces are fifteen hundred miles apart, I don't like it.'

She said, smiling: 'But that's worse for *them*, isn't it? We have the best communications network in the world, and theirs . . . '

'Yes. You're right, of course. But they outnumber us . . . who knows? Five hundred to one? A thousand to one? We'll never know their real strength, not even after we've knocked them on their arses. That's the kind of operation this is, we're cutting off the head and the arms, and we'll never know how strong the rest of the body was. Because the body is Indian, and as far as we're concerned, it's inviolable. I hope everyone understands that.'

'They understand that.'

He was lying on his belly, naked, as she stood above him and massaged his shoulders, her hands firm and strong as a man's, her talent expert. She wore the short blue wrap-around robe, and looking down at her legs he thought they went on and on and on forever, the longest legs in the world, and well-formed too. He ran a hand over her thigh, as smooth as silk, her own flesh almost as hard as his own.

She said: 'All right, roll over.'

He rolled on to his back and stared up at her, and she went to work on his pectoral muscles, kneading, stretching, pounding. Her fingers were strong on his thighs, and he could feel the blood

106

coursing faster. She rubbed him down with alcohol, and when she had finished held out his gown for him. He stood up and got into it, and said:

'I'd be lost without you, Charles. Get Betty de Haas for me, will you?'

'All right.'

'Have you checked out the radio?'

'Yes, I have. Suliman is here in case anything goes wrong.'

'Ah, good.'

Suliman was the new operator, a man of astonishing competence, a deserter from the Sudanese army, who had almost been shot because he'd refused to wipe out his own village at his Egyptian officer's demands.

She rolled up the sheet that was over the bamboo table they had been using, and collected the bottles and took them out, and Betty de Haas came in, her maps under her arm; he thought for a moment that he'd never – well, almost never – seen Betty de Haas without her maps, a woman who lived for cartography and dreamed of almost nothing else.

He said: 'Well, let's see what we've got.'

She unrolled the maps on the table, one on top of the other, already in the order in which she would use them; each one had a sheet of white paper clipped to it, closely filled with her own neat handwriting; there was nothing slap-dash about Betty de Haas, and she pulled out a chair for the Colonel, and sat down beside him when he had taken his seat.

She was like a teacher, making her points with precision and a certain didactic clarity. She said: 'What we are concerned with at this moment, is pin-pointing the logical place for Xira's *mestizo* army to be when he's ready to strike, in order that we ourselves may be in a better position to hit them. Now. Here, the area between the Itapixuna, where their main force is, and Gurupa, where they believe the Brazilian army to be. There's one thing we have to take note of. The National Geographic maps are incomplete, the Brazilian Naval charts show a great many discrepancies, and the charts of the Laresdes Expedition, generally considered to be the best, do not correspond very precisely with the latest aerial photographs which the Americans supplied to the OAS only four months ago. So . . . I have decided to use Confolens' old sketches as the master, and I only hope they're right.'

'If Confolens made them,' the Colonel said, 'they'll be right.'

'Yes. Yes, I believe so. All right, let's agree on that. Now . . .

the Itapixuna is deep and very fast-flowing all the way from here
. . . to here. But it can be crossed easily over a three-mile long
stretch here; the water is fast, but it's shallow. A lot of granite
and bluestone above the water, with the right flank protected by
a two-hundred-foot-high waterfall, and the left by a deep gorge
which can't be crossed at all, it's more than a mile wide. So, the
logical pin-point for them to select as their battle ground is
precisely . . . here. The army's made up of wild-rubber tappers,
they know this part of the jungle very well indeed, and they'll
arrive at the same conclusion as we do, through their own experi-
ence and expertise. We need a larger scale.'

She took away the top map and rolled it up carefully, and
pointed to the map below: 'They have two choices. Either they
can mount a small attack at this point, withdraw on the same
course back to point A, here . . . or they can bring the whole of
their army out into the plain at the bottom of this hill, and if
they do that, there's only one way for the Brazilians to react –
they'll have to move up on to the high country on either side of
them for flanking attacks, because they'll want to be above them.'

'Unless,' the Colonel said, 'they move down the defile, here. It
might give them the advantage of terrain.'

'No.' She was quite emphatic. 'The Xiristas would be running
the danger of getting the Brazilian army to the south of them,
they'll never allow that. On the plain, whatever time of the day
it might be, the sun will be favoring whoever is on the south,
there's no other way. Besides, if you follow the defile back a little,
you'll see it narrows down, here, to less than fifty feet. If they
want to retreat in a hurry, that's where they're going to be
trapped. They'd never allow that either.'

'Hold it.' The Colonel poured over the map for a while, studying every contour. 'What's this yellow here?'

'Quicksand. Just under three square miles of it.'

He studied the map again. 'Yes, you're right. Go on.'

'So, if we allow the Xiristas the military competence you suggest they have . . . '

He couldn't help smiling at the way she placed the onus for
the decision squarely in his lap. He said: 'Oh, they're competent
all right. Go on.'

'Then we can place them with a certain amount of accuracy.
They will keep their force together, rather than split up, because
of the Indians, and that's very good for us. And the Indians . . .
have got to be here.'

'Why?'

'They won't fight in pampas grass, they're more at home in the jungle. And they've got to have deep water behind them, so that if they want to turn and run, they can't. It's the only logical place for them to be placed. As soon as the Brazilians hit the Indians, the *mestizo* army can move out and regroup, either on the two flanks, or on one of them.' She looked at him and said: 'I think that's a decision you'll have to make yourself, the conditions are approximately the same whichever they do.'

'A strong probability they'll want their army intact, in one piece, but let me think about that. This river, the Pacaja Grande, can we ford it?'

'No. It's forty feet deep for more than a hundred and twelve miles. If you want to cross it you've got to move further upstream . . .'

'Where *we* will have the sun in our eyes.' He stubbed at the chart and said: 'Here, what's the width at this point, it doesn't look to be too much. Thirty feet?'

'A little less. And yes, there are trees right down to the edge, you can sling ropes over. I take it you won't want to be carrying bridges?'

'No, we'll use ropes. All right, let's make the battleground *here*. As soon as they start moving in for their feint attack, that's when we'll hit them.'

'And their retreat?'

The Colonel said: 'They won't retreat. We won't be as strong as the Brazilian army they're expecting, and they'll assume it's no more than a probe on their flanks.' He thought about it for a while, then: 'Well, perhaps we're giving them credit for too much expertise . . . all right, we'll have a small force sneak in behind them, between them and the Indians.'

'And if the Indians attack them?'

The Colonel said heavily: 'Yes, that's always the danger, isn't it? The last thing in the world that I want is a fight with the Indians. I've no intention at all of saving them – by destroying them.'

Charles was at the door, a tray of drinks in her hands. She came over and put it down on the table and said: 'A convoy coming in, they'll be here in a few minutes.'

'Bramble?'

'Yes, sir. Bramble, and Paul, and Rick Meyers, and Captain Duyvel.'

The Colonel looked at her: 'All of us together, that's what we've been waiting for with the Xiristas, isn't it? All of *them* together? I am wondering if they're waiting to blow our heads and arms off too?'

There wasn't much chance of it. There was no reason to suppose that Juan Xira even knew of their presence. And the scouts were there around the compound, constantly on the move, three jeeps out in the fields and two more men in the tall trees.

Colonel Tobin took the glasses and went to the verandah. Across the rolling green country, flat and fertile as far as he could see, with cattle grazing and a group of gauchos riding hard in the far distance, the long road ran, a dirt road of red gravel on which three open trucks were travelling, the dust a red plume behind them.

Through the high-powered naval glasses, he could see Paul in the lead truck, with Rick Meyers at his side. Bramble and Duyvel were following on behind, and the third truck, save for the driver, was empty. Far, far away, so small a speck that he could barely make it out, the plane that had brought them here was sitting in the middle of the wide pampas.

He turned away from the verandah, and said happily: 'All right, Charles, pour the Irish.'

As he waited, he looked at Betty de Haas and thought how admirable she looked in the khaki safari-shirt with the sleeves rolled up; it made her look like a school-girl just out of camp. He said: 'Are you putting on a little weight, Betty? Too much of that *churrasco*?'

She colored a trifle. 'No. I just . . . just left off some of my underwear, that's all.'

'Bram sees you without a bra, he's going to pounce on you. He's been after you for a long time.'

She sniffed. 'I'm quite sure I can handle Major Bramble.'

'Don't be too rough with him, he's a very nice fellow.'

She colored a trifle more; was he mocking her? 'Yes. Yes, I know that too.'

'Not fair to keep him waiting too long, you know. Sooner or later he's going to get you. I've a suspicion he promised himself that a long time ago.'

She gathered up her maps and said nothing. Charles was watching them, smiling faintly. She had changed from her robe into her field outfit again, the khaki bush-jacket and trousers, with the suede ankle-boots he liked so much, not too flat and yet still efficient. She was placing the chairs around the table now, and she looked at the ship's clock on the wall, brought from the Colonel's house in London, and murmured:

'Rio will be coming in in ten minutes' time, Tapajos fifteen minutes after that.'

'Good. Thank you, Charles. Tell Suliman to handle it, unless there's anything of importance, we don't want to be disturbed. Have him tell them to use the screamer-crystals from now on in, and I want him on the set for twenty-four hours a day.'

'Yes, sir.'

She went out, and when she came back, the others were with her, Paul and Bramble and Meyers and Duyvel, the High Command of the Private Army. They sat around the table in their accustomed order, with the Colonel at the head, Charles a little behind him to one side, then Paul, Rick Meyers. Duyvel, Bramble, and Betty de Haas on the Colonel's left. Their glasses were poured, the note-pads and pencils in place, and the Colonel said: 'All right, let's get down to business. First of all – Rio. What's happening, Rick?'

Meyers' dark, shrewd face was alive with excitement. He said: 'Alacrimo . . . is dead. He was shot and killed by the police this morning. He was on his way to the airport, en route to Tapajos with Juan Xira's sealed orders for the battle. Our man, Jorge Braga, was with him, and one of their men too, a man named Falares. Braga and Falares got the papers from him before he died, before the police picked him up, and they are on their way to Santarem in Tapajos now.'

Charles was looking at the Colonel, sure that he wasn't going to like it. The Colonel held up a hand, leaned back in his chair, and thought for a moment. He said at last, slowly:

'That sounds like a stroke of astonishingly good fortune, Rick. You know how much I hate it when good luck starts working for us. It's usually put there by someone else.'

Meyers was smiling: 'Not this time, Colonel. Braga told us in time, and we tipped off the police.'

'And Falares?'

'Falares is a nobody, just one of *them*. He and Braga had been detailed as bodyguards for Alacrimo, and that wasn't luck either. We had the police pick up his regular bodyguards at a time when we knew Braga would be coming to see him – it was a question of timing. Less than an hour to go for the plane, a missing body-guard . . . and Braga was there. It was perfectly logical for him to be detailed.'

'Braga has been with them for merely a matter of weeks, I don't like it.'

'They've investigated the background we gave him, and he

came out smelling like a rose.'

The Colonel looked at his son. 'Paul?'

Paul nodded: 'I'm perfectly happy with it, sir. A sequence of purely logical events, which we organised.'

'Does Xira know of Alacrimo's death?'

Paul shrugged: 'By now, without a doubt.'

'And he knows that Braga and this man Falares have the sealed orders?'

'Yes, he's sure to. It's certain that he's got spies at the airport. And when the police found nothing on Alacrimo's body, he'll take it for granted that either Braga or Falares has it.' He was very sure of himself. 'Otherwise, there could have been no reason for them to have gotten on the plane.'

'But he'll still make sure. He'll run a check on Braga again.'

'Maybe. And it'll still stand up, it's as solid as a rock.'

The Colonel said slowly: 'I am assuming that you had to tell the police that Braga was our man . . . otherwise he would have been in danger of getting shot himself.'

'No sir. We told Braga to expect a pick-up at the airport. We told him the police knew Alacrimo was there. And we told the police that Alacrimo would be alone. They knew that his body-guards had been arrested a short while before, and they had no way of knowing that in that short while, Braga and Falares had been detailed to take their place.'

He thought it over again. Then: 'Bramble?'

'I'm satisfied, sir.'

'All right, Rick. Go on.'

Meyers said: 'As soon as Braga gets to Tapajos, one of Duyvel's men will be there to get rid of Falares. They'll open the envelope, photograph the contents, reseal it, and Braga will take it then to Santarem, who's commanding the Xirista army. The copies of the orders will be flown back here as soon as possible – the plane is standing by to bring them here.'

The Colonel said: 'Well, we've just decided what those orders will be. But it's good to get corroboration, nonetheless.' His eyes were on Betty de Haas.

She said tartly: 'We'll merely be confirming that their sense of strategy is as good as ours.'

'Yes, I suppose that's so.' He said to Rick Meyers: 'And by the looks in your eyes, you've got something else up your sleeve, haven't you?'

Meyers nodded. Was he unsure of himself now, the Colonel

wondered? It was hard to see behind those shrewd, sometimes elusive eyes.

'Yes, sir, indeed we have. I've been studying some tapes that Jorge Braga got of a meeting with the Xirista High Command. Xira has called a meeting again at a place he calls the *papagaio de papel* for eleven o'clock on Wednesday night, at which time and place the signal will be given for the uprising to start. Xira will be there, with Juliao, who's the bomb expert, and Ajuda, who's the man chiefly responsible for all those kidnappings, and Arrifana, the planning expert, the man who decides who is going to be killed, and how, and when. At that meeting, Xira himself will detonate the explosives, by radio signal, that seem to me to be enough to blow up half the city. He'll then have a pre-recorded speech played over the two main radio stations, the others having been blown up, and announce the battle that by then will be going on between the Brazilian army in the north and his own *mestizos*. And finally, Arrifana is better known as Brigadier Alfonso da San Andres Lorenzo, and he's the number three man at the Ministry of Defense. He's been secretly with the Xiristas for over a year now, and he's the man who arranged for their use of Security Guard uniforms and papers when they kidnapped General Faleira.'

There was a long silence, and the Colonel said at last, very gently: 'I'm waiting for you to tell me what and where the *papagaio de papel* is. From your reluctance to mention it, I assume that you don't know that.'

Meyers sighed. Was he in for a bad time? He hoped not.

Paul came to his rescue and said: '*Papagaio de papel*, a paper parrot, it's also the word for a kite. No, I'm afraid we don't know where, or what that is. Not yet.'

'So we've got them at last, all together, the way we've always wanted them, only we don't know where.' The Colonel's tone was hard.

Paul said: 'Yes, I'm afraid that's true. We've got till Wednesday to find out.'

'And with Jorge Braga in the north, how do you propose to do that?'

Paul spread his hands wide: 'I simply don't know, sir. I just . . . don't know. I have one or two leads, Rick has a couple.'

'Wednesday, Paul. It all hinges on that now.'

'Yes. Yes, I know that.'

The Colonel held his look. He sighed. He said at last: 'All right, Major Bramble, I want you to take over the Northern

Force. As soon as Braga's report comes in, you may know more than we know now, but we've got enough anyway. Betty de Haas will brief you. Duyvel will be your second in command. Duyvel?'

The young Captain said: 'All ready, Colonel. We're just waiting for orders to move.'

'Total strength?'

'One hundred and four men all told. We lost one man, Heinneman, and we have seven wounded badly enough to be out of action.'

'Ah, Heinneman, yes I heard about that. I've been wondering if you need any heavy artillery?'

'No sir, I'd be happier without it.'

'I have seven twenty-five-pound gun Howitzers in the harbor at Sao Luis, and four of the new light weight eighty-eights. I can have any or all of them air-lifted for you in sixteen hours.'

Duyvel shook his head: 'We won't need them, sir.'

The Colonel looked at Bramble: 'Do you concur?'

'Yes sir. I agree with Duyvel.'

'All right.'

The Colonel never interfered with the plans of his commanders in the field. It was a matter of principle. He kept an eye on them, guided them, sometimes reprimanded them . . . but once the battle was on, they were in charge.

He said: 'All right, Bramble and Duyvel in the north, Major Tobin and Captain Meyers in Rio. And Paul . . . find that *papagaio*. It's no good wiping out their army, if they're going to wipe out half the capital. And I want . . .'

There was a stylised knock on the door, and Charles said swiftly: 'It's Suliman. I'll see.'

They waited while she went to the door and disappeared. She came back in a moment and said: 'It's Confolens, on the radio from Rio. They've just received word, all the Brazilian troops are back in their bases.'

The Colonel nodded: 'Good. Then the field's open for us. When can I expect those orders from Braga?'

Duyvel said: 'Any time now, Colonel.' He looked at his watch. 'Braga touched down at Tapajos an hour and a half ago. The plane that's standing by is a Bellanca, it shouldn't take more than fifty minutes to get here.' He said again: 'Any time now.'

'Then all we can do . . . is wait. Bramble, get together with Betty, she'll go over the charts with you and show you what your battle-field looks like. All dependent, of course, on corroboration from Jorge Braga, but we're fairly sure we've got it all worked

114

out.' He said blandly: 'Better use her room, it's quieter there, you won't want to be disturbed.'

He saw that Betty was looking at him, grave and very cool, her head tilted back slightly; Bramble was trying not to look too pleased.

He watched them go out together, then took his son by the arm and shepherded him out on to the verandah, down the steps and on to the lush grass, and along the red-dust track that bisected the bright green plantings. They walked for an hour, and when the sun was beginning to sink, a crimson ball of fire in the deep blue sky, with small white clouds of cumulus drifting by, they heard the Bellanca roaring in.

It swooped low over their heads and they looked back and saw Charles standing there, the finder in her hand, tapping out the recognition signal. They saw the package come floating down on its little red parachute, and Paul ran to retrieve it and gave it to his father, and they went back into the house and studied it.

They sat together at the bamboo table, and as the Colonel finished with the photographed sheets one by one, he passed them over to Paul, and Charles sat there and waited, and the Colonel said to her at last: 'Get Major Bramble and Betty for me, will you, Charles?'

She went and fetched them in, and the Colonel handed Bramble the pages and said: 'Now we'll find out if your Portuguese is as good as you pretend.'

He waited a while as Bramble read on, and looked at Betty and said: 'They've chosen their battleground. It's precisely where you said it would be. And their order of battle is exactly as you predicted. Exactly.'

Her face was flushed; he wondered which of the pleasures had given it its color. He looked at Bramble and said affably: 'She's worth her weight in gold, isn't she?'

Bramble said, beaming: 'She is indeed, solid gold.' His face was flushed too.

The Colonel looked at Betty, and winked.

CHAPTER ELEVEN

SAO SEBASTIAO
Co-ordinates: 22.54S. 43.18W.

The lovely old house in Sao Sebastiao, built by one of the rubber barons more than a hundred and eighty years ago, was in darkness when they arrived. But at the faint sound of the Buick as it purred smoothly up the long driveway, the lights were going on, first in the upper part of the house on the eastern side, then in the lower hallway, and finally on the broad, trellised patio entrance itself. The dogs, chained, were baying.

The headlights were playing over the purple clematis, the blood-red hibiscus, the night-blooming jasmine, and the yellow honeysuckle that scented the air so strongly he could almost believe it was her perfume.

He pulled to a stop and switched on the interior light, and turned to look at her, leaning back against the door and wondering. Her face was white, the enormous eyes dark and reddened with her crying. He had told her about the General's death; not about the mutilations, she could learn that later, and not from him. The sharp arch of her brows came together, a frown of . . . was it anger? Or merely anxiety? Was it for her dead General, or was it, perhaps for him? She wore a simple black dress that Nicola had brought her, and her legs were bare, the toe-nails dark red, red as her lips, in the open-toed black sandals.

He said quietly: 'You must pull yourself together, Estrella. I need you now.'

She took a deep, shuddering breath: 'I'll be all right. Be patient with me, Paul . . . I told you I didn't love him, you remember? Perhaps . . . I don't know, perhaps I truly did. Now that he's gone . . . I just don't know any more.'

He said again: 'I'm depending on you now. You know what you have to do.'

'Yes, I know.'

'A sense of urgency until she tells us.'

'And if she doesn't?'

116

Paul shrugged: 'There's no reason why she shouldn't. Start the ball rolling, then leave it to me.'

'And you won't harm her?'

'No, of course not. Are you ready?'

'Yes, I'm ready, as ready as I ever shall be.'

'Urgency, remember that.'

The front door was opening already, and Maria Josinara was there, the maid who took messages to Juan Xira. She wore a long woollen coat over her nightdress, and her hair was in curlers. A small, dark, girl, quite attractive, a little plump, about twenty years old. She was holding the coat tight at her throat, though the night was warm, and when she saw Paul she touched a hand to her curlers and gasped, and said: '*Tenho muita pena,* I'm sorry, I didn't expect . . . '

Estrella swept past her, regally. 'It doesn't matter, Maria. Come with us, into the living-room.'

The maid closed the door behind Paul, looking at him covertly, and followed them through.

The room was large, oak-panelled, with furniture of dark ebony and velvet in blues and greens, with long heavy drapes of gold velour. Estrella was pulling them tightly closed, and she said, not looking back: 'This is Paulo, Maria. He's one of us. It's urgent we get a message to Juan Xira. Do you know where he is?'

She swung round then, looking at the young girl closely. Watching her, Paul thought: The deviousness is there, drilled into her . . .

Maria shook her head: 'Senhor Xira? No, I do not know where he is, he might be anywhere.'

'He's in town, he's got to be.'

'Perhaps, I simply don't know.'

Paul looked at Estrella. He said tightly: 'We've got to find him, in the next twenty-four hours, or the whole organisation is going to get blown open, just when we're on the verge of success.'

'I know.' She turned back to Maria. 'When I give you messages for him,' she said, 'where do you take them?'

Maria shrugged: 'Sometimes to the house on Rua Magalaes, or to the place on *Morro de Canagolo*, or the lookout tower. Or sometimes to the café on Rua Tubira. If he is expecting a message, he usually lets me know, one way or the other, where he can be reached.'

The arch over those glorious, vivid eyes was coming together again, a frown of impatience: 'The café on Rua Tubira?'

'Yes. One of the waiters there is with us.'

'I don't think I know it. What's it called?' Her tone was very level. Paul was waiting, letting her carry it along.

Maria said: 'Sandal's Café, the one at the end of the road. But he's not there now, the waiter, he's gone north with Santarem.'

Paul said slowly: 'In case of a real emergency, where would you take a message? If you didn't know where he was, but had to find him?'

The maid turned to look at him, her face open and frank and very young. 'Well, I don't really know, *eu nao sei nada*. I would go, I think, to *Morro de Canagolo*, to the cellar where they meet sometimes.' She smiled, a quick, alert sort of smile, and touched her hand to her hair again and looked at her mistress and said: 'May I take these off? If I had known you had company . . .'

'Yes, of course, my dear.'

Estrella sat down and crossed her legs, and looked at Paul while the maid let down her hair, long black hair that fell to her waist, not yet properly waved, but shining like the wing of a blackbird, a blue sheen to it.

She tossed the hair behind her and said: 'In daylight, I would go up to the tower to look for someone, but you can't get there in the dark very easily, it's a very dangerous road. I never did like heights. No, at night, I would go to the *Morro*, the janitor there could pass on a message.' She looked at Paul and said, blushing: 'His name is Paulo, too.'

He remembered the tower now, the old lookout that had been built in the 1550's, when the Huguenots had tried, with not much success, to establish a colony on the Bay of Rio de Janeiro. It hung high in the air on the edge of the cliff, a wild bird perched there, a predator overlooking the whole of the beautiful bay, with two great concrete wings on either side of it, built into the mountain to catch the rain-water and channel it into cisterns.

A predatory bird perched on the edge of the cliff . . . He could feel his scalp tingling.

He said: 'Ah yes, the lookout tower, what do they call it?'

The maid shrugged, a nervous, incisive gesture: 'It's called the *Torre do Comando*, the Command Tower.' She smiled. 'But Juan always calls it the *papagaio de papel*, the paper kite. I always think it looks more like a *borboleta*, a butterfly.'

He felt that Estrella's eyes were on him, and he avoided looking at her. He said lightly: 'Well, it's got to be the *Morro* . . . how long will it take you to get there?'

She shrugged: 'Two hours, a little more.'

'All right. First thing in the morning, I want you to take an envelope with you and go there . . . '

Estrella interrupted him: 'She should go tonight, Paulo. It is better.' She was carefully not looking at him, and he said slowly: 'Yes, perhaps it is better that you go tonight.'

Estrella got to her feet and went to the cupboard and found coffee cups, and said to the maid: 'Put on water for the coffee before you get dressed. I will see to it when it's ready.'

'*Sim, Senhora.*' The girl threw a quick glance at Paul and went out, and he said, wondering if he knew the answer already: 'Why, Estrella?'

'Don't you know why? I'm sure you must.'

She would still not meet his eye. She was putting the cups down on the dark table, a silver bowl of sugar with them. She said, and there was an elegant lift of those slender shoulders:

'We told her there was an urgent message, a sense of urgency, your own words. If you tell her now that tomorrow will do, she may suspect something is not right.' She was moving the cups again, setting them just so, the china tinkle a fragile sound in the quiet room. 'And now that you know where the *papagaio* is . . . '

She turned to look at him, her eyes holding his. He said slowly: 'I thought perhaps there might be another reason. I hoped there was another reason.'

She turned away again, and smoothed the dress down over her pointed breasts, a sensuous, deliberate movement. She took some tiny spoons from a velvet-lined box, and put two of them in the saucers, and said very quietly: 'I wanted her out of the house for the night. Does that make you angry?'

'No. I'm very glad. If that's what you really want.'

'Yes, that's what I want. And you?'

'More than you can imagine. Yes, I want.'

He walked over to her, and she held out her arms for him, and he held her tight and kissed her, feeling the warmth of her body tight against his, her waist so narrow that he could not believe it, her hard breasts firm against his chest.

He said wryly: 'It would be wrong for me to say I love you, wouldn't it? Will you accept less than that?'

'Yes, I will accept what you have for me. Love, or desire, or . . . anything else. If you will say only that you want me . . . '

'Oh God, I want you.' He strained himself to her again, feeling her gentle writhing, and when they heard Maria returning they stood a little apart and waited for her.

The girl came into the room and said: 'The kettle is on the

119

stove, *Senhora*, and I should be back by . . . oh, four o'clock.'

'Good. Try not to be too late, Maria. Paulo will stay here to-night, is the guest-room ready?'

'Ready, *Senhora*, but not aired. Shall I see to it before I go?'

'No. I will do it.'

Paul was sitting at the table, writing a note on the pad there. He found some envelopes in the drawer and sealed the sheet of paper in it, and handed it to Maria and said: 'Which way will you go?'

'I will take the bus from the corner to Lagoa Rodrigo, and then I can walk.'

'Along the lakeside?'

'Yes, the Avenida Epitacio.'

'All right. Be careful, Maria.'

She was slipping the note into the top of her black stockings, the white skin gleaming. 'I will be careful.'

'*Esta bem. Ate logo.*'

They waited till she had gone and they had heard the front door close behind her, and then Estrella was in his arms again, holding herself close against him. He disengaged himself gently and said:

'One more thing, first . . . '

He went to the phone and said: 'I hope it's working. If not, we're in trouble.'

'Yes, yes, it's working.'

He dialled the number, let it ring three times, then rang off and dialled again, their code, and said: 'Nicola? Can you talk?'

Estrella was at the door, a heightened color to her white cheeks, her eyes very bright. 'How do you like your coffee, Paul?'

'Very strong, but not too sweet.' They made coffee in these parts by first filling the cup with sugar. On the phone, Nicola's voice was very low, very alluring: 'Yes, Paul, I can talk, I'm alone, I'm in bed.'

'Check the line for a tap, and call me back right away at 751-572. Have you got the box handy?'

'Yes. In sixty seconds.'

He put down the phone and waited, and when it rang again he let the buzzer sound for sixty seconds and then picked it up.

Nicola said: 'Everything checks out, the line's okay. Go ahead, Paul.'

The scent of the coffee was coming to him out of the kitchen, a fine, domestic kind of smell.

He said: 'The midnight bus from Sao Sebastiao, it gets to the

Avenida Epitacio Pessoa at twelve forty-five or thereabouts. There's a girl on it, a young girl in a brown checked woollen coat, twenty years old, black hair, heavy black shoes with brass buckles on them, are you with me?'

'Yes, I'm here.'

'She mustn't get where she's going. And she mustn't be harmed, either. Just keep her under wraps till further notice. All right? Get Confolens if you think it's necessary, or one of the boys, maybe Efrem Collas. Call me back as soon as you're through, will you do that? Let me know where you're holding her, and how she is. Get a message through to the old man for me, tell him we've found the item we were looking for. And finally . . . you know the *Torre do Comando*?'

'Yes, I know it.'

'What goes on there? Isn't it deserted?'

'Yes, it has been for a long time, thirty years or more, what's on your mind?'

'I want a plan of it, first thing in the morning. Try the Military Museum. A floor plan, sketches, anything you can find, I'll get them from you tomorrow.'

'All right. Where are you now?' she asked. 'Your telephone prefix is Sao Sebastiao, isn't it?'

An inquisitive woman, Nicola . . .

He said: 'Yes, that's where I am for the rest of the night.'

'Anything?'

Paul said: 'Nothing, Nicola. Just hoping for a good night's sleep, on and off, that's all. But call me back, let me know. G'night, Nicola.'

'Right.'

He put down the phone as Estrella came back into the room with the coffee-pot on a carved oak tray. She had found time to change into a white silk negligee, the white and gold that suited her so well. She put down the tray and sat down close beside him, and put her hand in his, and put a hand to his sunburned cheek and stroked it gently: 'Will you promise me one thing, Paul? Will you promise me?'

'If I can . . .'

'Will you forget about the General?'

'Have *you* forgotten him, Estrella?'

'No. No, not really. But that's not the same thing, is it? But I'm not . . .' Her eyes were turned away now; she set her negligee just so and said, slowly: 'A mistress is not a whore, Paul. I'm not . . . not a whore.'

121

'I know that.'

'He was the first man in my life, the only man. Till now. And I'm asking myself if . . . if it's just *somebody* I need. Or *you.*'

'Can you make believe at least that it's me?'

'Oh Paul . . . yes, I can, I truly can . . .'

He pulled her across his lap and ran his hands over her body, caressing her small, naked breasts, running his hands along her thighs. And in a little while, they left the coffee to get cold there on the great oak table, and turned out the lights, and went upstairs to her room.

He woke at two in the morning at the sound of the telephone ringing, and left her warm body there, sleeping, and went downstairs to answer it.

It was Nicola. 'Can you talk, Paul?'

'Yes, I can talk.'

'We've got her. She's with Confolens at the safe house. And she's all right. Mad as hell, but all right.' There was a laugh at the other end. 'She bit his hand, clear through to the bone, a virago.'

'All right, keep her there till you hear from me.'

'She was carrying a damn great hand-grenade under her blouse, did you know that?'

'No, I didn't.'

'And a rather cryptic message, a note that said: *the waters in the basin are rising . . .*'

'That, I know about. Just a lot of gobbledygook, it doesn't mean a thing. Good-night, Nicola. Sleep well.'

She said wistfully: 'I don't suppose you'd be coming over here tonight?'

'Er, no . . . I hadn't thought of it. What's on your mind?'

'Nothing, Paul. Just a thought. Good-night.'

When she had rung off, Paul looked at the receiver and said to himself: 'Well, I'll be damned.'

He put back the phone and went upstairs, and woke Estrella and made urgent love to her again, the moonlight streaming in through the open window now, the scent of the jasmine coming in over the verandah. And when they were both exhausted, he lay beside her with one hand on her breast and one on that tight smooth stomach, and slept.

CHAPTER TWELVE

SERRA DA CARIOCA.
Co-ordinates: 22.52S.   43.18N.

The great tower reached so high that it seemed to dwarf even the huge concrete statue of Christ on top of Corcovado Mountain beyond it. It was a towering, circular building of rough-hewn stones, some of them crumbling now, with a perilous wooden stairway running up its inside wall.

The wide concrete slopes at either side, that were the water-cachement area, stretched out for more than a thousand feet, the wings of some huge, ungainly bird, of which the tower itself was the long and scraggy neck.

From the beach so far below, it seemed infinitely small; up here, it was tremendous, perched high on the edge of a cliff that was itself so high that you could see, from its lip, for more than fifty miles in all directions. And from the top of the tower, another four hundred and eighty feet . . .

Waiting in the darkness, Paul began to work it out in his head; the time was passing slowly. The distance in sea-miles, he was thinking, equals one point one seven times the square root of the height in feet above sea level, all the old instructions from the detailed sessions at the training school, with refresher courses in between operations to keep the members of the Private Army at the peak of their considerable efficiency. Sixty-two point four miles, then, a gigantic saucer nearly a hundred and twenty-five miles across.

Did Xira derive, perhaps, his sense of power from this strange vantage-point? *All the land that I see, I will destroy* . . .

Beside him, in the darkness, Confolens whispered: 'Arrifana.'

Paul took the infra-red night-glasses from him, and studied the figure that was moving quickly among the trees and heading for the tower: 'Arrifana, and two other men behind him, their sub-machine-guns not very carefully concealed, and why should they be? Who would see them here in this deserted pinnacle of the forested mountain?

He said: 'The others?'

'No, just Arrifana. The others are bodyguards.'

He watched Arrifana go to the door and unlock it, saw the huge teak door swing open, the rusting hinges oiled for silence, and heard the sound of the lock being turned again from the inside.

Confolens said: 'You can't use your blaster on the lower door.'

'I know it.'

The blaster was in his satchel, a fearsome weapon.

Confolens had thrown back his head, was mentally counting the paces of the long, hard climb to the top. He said at last: 'There, a light.'

Paul swung the binoculars up and looked. Yes, a pale gleam of light seeping through what looked like canvas drapes over the castellated window of the circular guard-room at the top. From any but this close angle, it would not be visible. He said: 'The guard-room, then, just as we reckoned.'

The sketches had shown it clearly, the floor-plan even more so, in the report from the Bureau of Maintenance of Public Monuments that Nicola had brought him.

' . . . and the guard-room is still habitable, the only room in the building that remains suitable for use, though the cellar might perhaps, with considerable expenditure, be rendered useful . . . all the stairs were found serviceable, except for the seventy-second, the eighty-first, and the ninetieth, which are broken . . . '

The report was less than a year old.

How long had Xira been coming here, to brood over the land he wanted to claim, staring out across the wide panorama with hatred smouldering in his eyes? Was his need for symbolism a weakness?

Confolens said: 'There, on the path.' Paul turned the glasses there, and watched, and handed them to Confolens, and Confolens said in a moment: 'Juliao and Ajuda, that's three of them now. Santarem's in Tapajos, Alacrimo is dead . . . the only one we're waiting for is Xira himself.'

Paul was squirming in the silence, fidgeting restlessly. Through the heavy foliage, he could see the splendid backdrop of Rio, a million lights down there, a city ostensibly at peace; but with countless buildings mined for destruction, the fires sweeping through the chaos and burning, burning, burning . . . and with the detonating device up there in that great round room above them somewhere, an hour to go before the madman would throw the switch and start an inferno of mayhem. He thought of the bleeding, screaming, bodies down there in the rubble . . .

He said: 'Two minutes to twenty-two hundred hours, I don't like it at all.'

'Oh?' He could feel Confolens' eyes on him in the darkness.

'A feeling, nothing more, it doesn't smell right. Get Collas for me, will you?'

Confolens glided away, and came back in a moment, two shadows now, moving in silence.

Paul whispered: 'Where's Cass Fragonard?'

Collas pointed: 'Over there, under the bushes. Five men, now, have walked right past him. We know who they are?'

'Arrifana, Juliao, Ajuda, and two bodyguards. We're still waiting for Xira.'

'Any chance he might be in there already?'

Paul said heavily: 'Yes, it's a possibility. This could be his regular hideout. We've been watching since dark and seen nothing, and that doesn't mean a goddam thing. Roberts?'

'On the other flank, watching the west side, with Manuel.'

'We'll give him another half-hour. I'm not going to sit out here waiting for Xira and find that he's changed his plans, that someone else is going to throw that damned switch . . .'

He said to Confolens: 'At half-past ten, I'm going in. Now, if Xira hasn't come by then, you'll have to wait outside. Give me four minutes to get to the top, and in those four minutes I've got to have silence, so . . . if Xira turns up, you kill him silently, and I don't care if he's got fifty bodyguards with him, I've got to have silence. The sound of a single shot, and one of the men in there is going to panic and blow up half the town. When I go in . . .' He said grimly: 'You'll know when the coast is clear.' He turned to Collas. 'Tell the others, then come right back. I want you and Cass Fragonard with me, Roberts and Manuel with Confolens outside. Clear?'

'Clear.'

'Go pass it on.'

They waited. Paul whispered at last, feeling the need to say something: 'One of the reasons Xira has stayed alive so long: his movements are unpredictable.'

'When Alacrimo was killed . . . ?'

'Yes, that's what I was thinking. If Alacrimo was carrying verbal messages as well as those sealed orders . . . yes, it's possible Xira has gone north to Tapajos, to join Santarem for the final showdown. If so . . . we improvise.'

125

And improvisation, they would reiterate in the School, is what half of military strategy is about. You plan, and you have a contingency, and if that doesn't work either, you use your own initiative, that's what you're being trained for . . .

He looked at his watch again: 'Ten more minutes.'

Collas and Fragonard were there beside him; he had not heard them come in. He said, his voice very low: 'Five men in there, perhaps more. I want them dead in the first two seconds. And somewhere in that room, there's a detonator box, an array of buttons . . . I haven't the vaguest idea what it looks like, or just where it's at. But God help anyone who puts a bullet in it. God help us all. That will be my job, and don't count on me for anything else. I'll get the door open, and then . . . then forget about me, just try not to blow my head off, wherever I am. Clear?'

Their eyes were bright, their faces blackened. Fragonard said to Collas: 'You take those left of center, I'll take the right, okay?'

'Check.'

Paul said, insisting: 'Single shots, no bursts. If one bullet ricochets and hits that detonator . . .'

'Okay, okay, don't worry about it.'

The minutes were ticking by. There was no sign of Juan Xira. Paul was staring at his luminous dial, counting the seconds, and with thirty more to go, he said, quickly, whispering: 'Four minutes of silence.'

He ran quickly to the door, worked on the lock for ten seconds with the skeleton key, went inside, and slowly, carefully, began to climb the stairway, the two others silent behind him, the long flight of narrow, narrow steps, no railing anywhere, that wound round and round and round the stone wall. He was remembering the report, the seventy-second, the eighty-first, the ninetieth steps, all broken; a slip could send them all hurtling down the well to the bottom again; they'd all seen the papers, spent two hours poring over them together, planning the assault.

Four hundred and thirty feet up into the darkness, winding round and round, feeling each step gently, not trusting the broken stones. Their rope-soled shoes were silent as they climbed steadily upwards, keeping in close to the wall, trying not to think of the long, deep, unprotected shaft that once, they knew, had housed the ropes and the winch that hoisted the watch-tower's guns up to the top.

The balustrade at last, thank God, and relative safety.

Paul reached out and tapped each man twice on the shoulder, Fragonard on his right, Collas on the left. The thought came to him, in a moment of incongruity, that it was very fitting. Collas had once been a militant Communist, Cass Fragonard a virulent Fascist; now they were both where they belonged, steadily in the center of the road, sweeping away the rubble on either side. The thought amused him.

They tapped him back twice, each in turn, and spaced themselves out on the narrow platform. Would the blast of the gun knock them all off it?

Lightly, delicately, he ran his finger-tips over the surface of the door. Wood . . .

The report had said: ' . . . *and a wooden door, Mark Two, General Services, should be fitted to the entrance to the guard-room to prevent unauthorised entrance, unless the Minister is of the opinion that the expense of a steel door would be justified . . .*'

He'd been unable, at such short notice, to find out; but he was ready for either. He took the reduced-action charge from his satchel, and replaced the armor-piercing shell in his PIAT, the Projector – Infantry, Anti-Tank that would blast, in its normal form, through four-inch armor. The weapon had been cut down, reduced in weight, and modified by the team of weapons specialists under Edgars Jefferson, their best man on missiles, till it was the next best thing to a hand-gun. He placed the muzzle against the door, held his body to one side to avoid the fierce anger of the recoil, and pulled the trigger.

The shell went off with a blast that, in the confined space, nearly blew them off their feet. The door was gone, a smouldering hole in its place, and he was racing through, dropping his weapon to leave both his hands free, racing across the wide, round room to the console that was against the opposite wall. Two of the men in there were racing towards it too, Ajuda and one of the guards, and he saw Ajuda go down with a single bullet through his head, and the guard swing round as Collas blasted him.

The console was under his hands, then, its row of eight buttons shining in the light of the four oil lamps that had been hung on the wall. He wrapped his body around it, hearing the sound of the rapid, controlled firing, searching out the wires and their connections, and a hand ripped at his face from behind and then was gone, leaving a trail of bloody scratches across his cheeks.

And then, there was silence. He had counted the shots; five, no more.

He looked around him. Collas and Fragonard were standing close to the doorway still, and there were five dead bodies on the floor; Juliao, Ajuda, two guards, and the Xirista who had become known as Arrifana but was really the third man on the list at the Ministry of Defense.

He could feel the faint tick of the console under his hands, and he said: 'My God, they've got automation . . . ' The pale green light of the illuminated dial showed 00.16.32, and the seconds were ticking away. It turned down to 31, 30, 29, 28, 27, 26 . . .

Paul said calmly: 'Collas, I think you had a course in these things, you're supposed to be our local expert. Where's the booby-trap likely to be?'

Collas was there, close beside him, a thin screwdriver ready. 'Here, we just loosen this screw . . . very gently . . . ' Paul left him to it, and Collas, working steadily, said: 'West German, a very efficient piece of machinery, timed to set off a radio signal at eleven o'clock precisely, that's fifteen and a quarter minutes from now. I need ten minutes to dismantle it. Can we have some more light?'

'Cass.'

Fragonard broke out the quartz-halogen battery-lantern, and flooded the guard-room with its brilliance. Paul ripped off the canvas that had been nailed over the castellated windows, and stared out across the bay, drawing in his breath at the spectacular panorama, the mountains dark under the bright moon, the silver sea shimmering far, far below them, so far down that it seemed they were up there with the gods.

He said: 'Get to it, Collas, or that lot's going to be blown sky high.'

Collas said: 'Booby-trap's out.' He heard the snip of the shears and turned back, and Collas was there grinning at him, the deck of the console in his hands. He lifted out a transistor and held it up, and said: 'This, this is all it is. Trigger this little baby, and yes, one hell of a lot of the town down there goes up in flames.' He dropped the transistor to the floor, and ground it to powder under his heel.

Paul said: 'All right, we've got three hours to get to Tapajos. Let's go find that plane. Let's go see if he knows how to take off in the dark, with no lights, no runway, no nothing. And let's hope, for God's sake, that he can.'

CHAPTER THIRTEEN

THE ITAPIXUNA
Co-ordinates: 05.01S. 53.28W.

The Bellanca, flying at twelve thousand feet, had cut its motors fifteen minutes ago, and was gliding lazily above the damp clouds.

The young pilot said cheerfully: 'You've all got to go together, unless you want me to start engines and make another run.' His name was Larna, and he came from Crete, and he could fly anything that had wings, with an expertise far beyond his twenty-four years.

Paul said: 'No, we go together.'

There were four of them hunched there, waiting; Paul Tobin, and Fragonard, and Collas and Roberts. The twenty-foot directional parachutes would take them down fast, and they hoped that Bramble had found a comfortable spot for them to land in.

Larna said: 'Finder locked in, four minutes to go.'

'Take us down to eight hundred.'

'Eight hundred coming up.' The Bellanca dived steeply, and banked, and turned round and steadied itself, and Larna said at last, watching the dials: 'He's dead ahead, about ninety seconds, check your straps.'

'Straps checked.'

'Stand by, coming in.'

The long row of green lights were flashing on, one each second; the tenth, and last, would be red.

Paul said: 'Let's make it pin-point, shall we?'

And Larna said sharply: 'Go!'

They jumped together, and as soon as the chutes were open, Paul looked around and saw, with satisfaction, the diamond pattern they had taken, not one of them more than twenty feet from his neighbor. They went down at an alarming speed, pulling on the cords and slicing through the damp air. Collas and Cass Fragonard were so close that their chutes were touching, and then they landed together and rolled over and pulled in on the cords, though there was no wind, and Bramble was standing there grinning at them, and saying:

'Well, it's nice to see you, how's Rio?'

Paul said: 'Rio is safe. But we didn't get Xira, he wasn't there.'

The grin widened. 'I know. He's here. Santarem sent Jorge Braga out on a probing mission, and he conveniently got lost and rejoined us. Seems that Xira flew in early this morning; they've got a helicopter, Naval.'

'Well, we'll just have to take it away from them, won't we?'

They were gathering up the parachutes, burying them in the sticky mud.

Major Bramble said: 'Your headquarters are a mile up the hill, Paul. Everything's ready to go.'

'My headquarters? Oh no.' Paul said cheerfully: 'You heard the Colonel, this is your battle, you're in command.'

Major Bramble was secretly pleased, but he nodded and said nothing.

They moved off under the bright moon together, climbing from the swamp up the side of the green mountain, and when they reached a point of vantage, they looked back at the valley, and Bramble said, pointing: 'Let me put you in the picture, at least.'

There were a million colors down there, even in the night. The rivers, the Itapixuna itself and all the streams that fed into it, were shining silver-bright; the patches of swamp were black, the gentle hills purple, the sandstone cliffs glowed with a dark opaque amber.

Bramble said: 'Along the bank of the river there, the Xirista army, as far as the scouts can tell, two groups of about three thousand each, separated by half a mile. Another two hundred men are moving now, along the line of the forest there, on a bearing of twenty-one degrees, more or less constant, and making a lot of noise. They've even got cooking fires going from time to time.'

'They're hoping the Brazilian army will move out, is what you figure?'

'As far as we know, they've every reason to believe the Brazilians are still there. They could have found out Colonel Tobin had them withdrawn, but Braga said no, they don't know that. So they are looking. They've slung ropes across the Itapixuna gorge, ready for a rapid retreat back to their main forces.'

'And the ropes, I take it . . . ?'

'Yes, Paul, they're no longer there. I've got forty-one archers

130

waiting for them to return, it seemed to me that silence would be effective . . . '

'They'll use their guns the moment your bowmen open up.'

'Of course. But it will all be over in a few moments. Just as long as we don't have the sounds of a full-scale battle.'

'Who's in charge of the archers?'

'Ahmed Idriss.'

'Good. Am I trying to run your battle for you?'

Bramble smiled; 'Anything you don't like the looks of, let me know, and we'll change it.'

'Go on.'

'The Indians are in the forest over there, an awful lot of them, but they're three miles back, which ought to give us enough room to operate. I've got the 4.2-inch mortars lined up in fox-holes flanking the line of the river, two thousand yards this side of it, and the 60mm. mortars eight hundred yards ahead of them. Two squads in reserve with knee-mortars on either flank, and two more with the MG42s behind them.'

The MG42s had a remarkable cycling rate of 1,200 rounds per minute, with an effective range of a touch over four thousand yards, a light-weight machine-gun that fired like a rifle on a bipod mount.

Bramble said: 'The Browning fifty-calibres are all on that hill there, at maximum range, seven thousand yards, that means they'll be shooting over everybody's heads and having a ball. Two squads standing by to cross the Itapixuna if they're required, and that's about it.'

'And you go into action . . . when?'

'Well, I *was* waiting for you, but . . . I'd say that by daylight, their advance guard will be sitting out in the open wondering what happened to the Brazilian army. How long they'll sit around, whether or not they'll push further forward, is anybody's guess, so I figured we'd start the attack at zero nine-hundred hours. By that time, I'm guessing that the men out on the probe will have discovered there's nothing there, and will be on their way back to the gorge, where they'll run right into our archers. Sure, they'll get off a few shots while they're being killed, but there is sporadic shooting all the time around here anyway.'

Paul said: 'I'm still worried about the Indians.'

'Don't be.' Bramble said, laughing softly: 'You heard about the stragglers Duyvel picked up?'

'Yes, one Sasanico Indian and his two women.'

131

'He attached himself to Blackman, our poor professor, and . . .'
He threw out his hands in a gesture. 'The man's name is
Alarihastu, which is Sasanico for He-Who-Gives. Very fitting.
He's given Blackman his daughter.'

'Oh my God.'

'A ritual Indian wedding, if you want to call it that. Purple
orchids, burned toucan feathers, porcupine quills, and the virginal
blood gathered in an armadillo shell, the whole schtik. And
Blackman is now standing by with his new family to sneak over
to the Indians and tell them that the Xirista army is about to turn
on them. He's quite sure, Blackman, that they'll simply fade
away into the jungle again, and take up their lives where they
left off, each man better off to the extent of one rifle.'

Paul said: 'Poor bloody Blackman. Are we saving ourselves
his guaranteed passage back home to London? Is he going to
spend the rest of his life in the jungle?'

Bramble shrugged. 'His problem, not ours. He doesn't seem
to be too concerned about it, he says . . . ' He was laughing again,
enjoying the thought of it. 'He says that all he has to do, and he's
the expert, remember, is to get the bride good and pregnant, bring
honor to the tribe, all that jazz. The way he's carrying on, I'd say
he's halfway to doing just that, he's at it day and night, you never
saw such a glutton.'

Paul sighed. 'All right, I've got three more men for you. Where
do you want them?'

Bramble said promptly: 'Collas with Ahmed Idriss, he could
do with another bowman, Roberts can take over the spare mortar,
the big one, 120mm., it's a hell of a baby to lug around, it'll get
rid of some of that paunch. Fragonard stays with us. Nine o'clock
in the morning all right with you?'

'Your battle, Bram.'

'Okay. Nine o'clock it is. Let's get over to Duyvel and tell
him the orders stand.'

They climbed slowly to the top of the great green hill, the
river shimmering in the moonlight there below them, and found
the command post where Captain Duyvel was waiting for them.
It was a twelve-foot tent that had been dug into the ground and
covered over with trailing begonias, and lantana, and amarylids,
and pink and yellow orchids that clambered loosely up into the
surrounding chocolate trees. A huge papaya tree, destroyed by a
creeping parasite, lay athwart the tent, and they bent low to
clamber underneath it, and Bramble said happily:

'Don't upset my camouflage too much, Paul, I'm very fond of begonias . . . '

In the steep red cliffs that framed the Itapixuna gorge, ten narrow slits had been cut, and buttressed with logs of soft palm-wood, then plastered over with red mud till they were quite invisible, five tiny man-made caves on each side of the deep river, commanding the point below them where the valley that led into it funnelled into its narrowest point.

There were four men in each of the caves, their bows ready, their loaded quivers slung over their right shoulder, each man with his own miniature radio and his binoculars placed on knife-cut ledges in front of him.

Above them, a tangle of creeping lantana was the camouflage under which Ahmed Idriss, the Libyan who had once been arch-ery instructor to the sons of the ruler, was sitting with his own command radio perched on his knees, his own bow on the ground in front of him. He squatted cross-legged under his camouflage, motionless, a desert Bedouin listening to the silence. He was staring out into the funnel of the valley, and he spoke quietly into the mike at his throat. He had taken off the high-impact helmet that was mandatory – if any of the senior officers was around – and had slung the receiver over his head on a wire brace. His eyes were unbelievably sharp.

He said, a whisper: 'They're coming in now. Study them, pick your targets, wait for the order to fire.'

Along the twin line of fox-holes, the men were peering out through the embrasures, watching the approaching column, a ragged line of heavily-armed *mestizos*, disgruntled now because the army they had been sent to look for just wasn't there. Some of them were drunk, but Paul had said: 'The *mestizo* is a fighting machine of astonishing competence, and when he gets drunk . . . he's more deadly, so watch out . . . '

Idriss said quietly into his mike: 'Ready your bows.'

The bows were all of yew, the old fashioned long-bow, each one made to his own individual measurements by the man who would use it, the yew-stave aged a minimum of eight years before it was carefully steam-straightened, sanded to size – the Colonel would not allow the use of cutting tools – and laboriously tillered into shape. Their arrows, each man also making his own, were of Port Oxford cedar brought specially for them from the island of Formosa, and the bow-strings were of Fortisan.

Idriss said, a touch of sarcasm in his voice: 'Six shafts to a

133

man should do it, anybody uses ten, he can get down there in the gorge and retrieve them. Neck shots, please, we don't want anyone firing back at us, all right for you children under cover, but I'm out here in the open.'

The column was moving steadily closer; he could see their faces clearly now. He said: 'Minimum range, eighty yards. Maximum, one hundred and thirty. Forget about the five men in front, I'll take them.' The five were the vanguard, moving a hundred and forty yards ahead of the others, far too close for safety. But even so, he was thinking, if the main body's in close ... he was calculating the distance, knowing he could handle it, two hundred and seventy yards, the Mongolian draw then, thumb around the bow-string ...

The column entered the gorge. He waited.

Now they were moving slowly between the two lines of caves He waited.

He said quietly: 'Open fire.'

His eyes were on cave three, directly opposite him on the other side of the narrow gorge; it would have been invisible had he not known where to look for it. He counted the arrows as they flew out, arching downwards at astonishing speed, four, eight, twelve, no massed flights here but single shafts following each other fast and accurately. Four more, and four more after that ... the men of the vanguard were turning back, staring up at the red cliffs in bewilderment, unsure of what was happening. The enemy they had been searching for was a myth, but here, where they knew they were safe ... some of the men in the main column were racing closer to the cliffs, running from one flanking fire into the other, and Idriss was thinking: it's always the trouble on the flanks that gets them, that and the surprise.

He picked up his bow in an almost leisurely fashion, eased his right shoulder for the quiver, and sent five long-range shots hurtling at the men out front, four neck shots and one in the chest; and they fell, and did not move again.

He heard a single rifle-shot, and looked quickly and saw that one man, an arrow through his thigh, was pointing his rifle blindly, and he sent a shaft quickly into his throat.

And then, the silence was acute. There had been a moment of shouting, a single shot, and then ... silence.

He sat quite still for a few moments, and studied the bodies down there for any sign of life; there was none. Routine now ... he said quietly: 'All right, shaft count please, by numbers.'

The voices came back to him, cave by cave, over the radio:

'Cave One, twenty-eight flights.'

'Two, twenty-two, Charlie broke his bloody bow-string.'

'Three, thirty-seven, we got a couple of amateurs in here.'

'Four, twenty-nine.'

'Five, thirty-one . . . '

The voices droned on. Two hundred and eighteen arrows all told, two hundred and four men dead on their battlefield. Casualties received, none. Elapsed time – eighteen seconds.

Idriss said into his mike: 'Hold your positions for ten minutes, then report back to Captain Duyvel for reassignment. Out.'

Phase One of the battle was over.

Radovic was on the mortars.

He had the four-point-two's; five-foot steel barrels rifled for accuracy that hurled a twenty-four-pound shell, flat-bottomed, for four thousand yards in sixty seconds. He had bullied his men to the point where they could send nine shells spinning into the air before the first one hit. He spoke over his radio to Hanson, on the sixties, eight hundred yards ahead of him. He said:

'I'm taking the center first. Give me three minuutes, then hit the flanks, put a nice bracket all round them.' He turned to Roberts, checking over the alignment of the big one-twenty. 'Two minutes after we open up, the knee-mortars go into action. That's your cue to give them a barrage four hundred yards behind the line of my burst, you've got the range.'

Roberts nodded: 'Just don't expect me to move this sonofabitch around too much, I got a hernia.'

Radovic was staring at the second-hand of his watch: 'Camouflage off, step on it.'

The men were hauling away the camouflage netting, piling the bushes out of the way. Rudi Vicek was at the photo-magnetic scanner, watching the needle of light swing round. He said: 'Man, they've got a lot of hardware down there, small stuff, mostly, but one hell of a lot of it.'

'Range, maximum and minimum.'

'Two thousand and eighty yards, two thousand and five. Bearings two-seventy-one to two-ninety-three for their right flank, thirty-eight to fifty-two degrees for their left. Left flank has eighteen heavy guns, right flank only eleven, and I think that's a 4.5 rocket-launcher down there, how come we never heard about that?' He stared at the flickering lights, dished the antenna to maximum, and said: 'No, by God, it's a couple of anti-tank

135

guns, wheel to wheel, I'd say they're thirty-seven millimetres. No, four of them.'

'All together?'

'Yes, very close.'

'Great. Give me the exact co-ordinates.'

Vicek studied his dials: 'Bearing thirty-nine point five two, range two thousand exactly.'

Radovic said: 'Okay, Roberts, swing your one-twenty over, you heard the man, I don't like anti-tank guns, they make too much noise.'

'Oh Christ.' With two of the men, Roberts swung the heavy mortar over on its massive steel base. 'Who the hell got this damn thing up here anyway?'

'Eight of us,' Radovic said, 'while you were sunning yourself on the beach at Copacabana. You want a picnic, you should have stayed there. One minute to go.'

The black box was beeping, and he threw the switch and said: 'Group Baker, go ahead.'

It was Bramble, up on the command post among the wild begonias: 'All ready down there?'

'Ready, sir.'

'All right. You may start firing in forty seconds from . . . now.'

The seconds were ticking away.

Radovic said: 'Fire!'

All around him, the four-point-twos burst into violent action as the men bent their bodies and passed over the shells, no one capping his ears, and someone shouted jubilantly: 'Ten in the air when that one hit . . . ' The din was deafening, the motions fast and mechanical.

Below them, in the long patch of dense jungle that was the enemy's hiding-place, they could see the bright red and yellow flashes where the shells burst. The anti-tank guns down there were opening up, the shells lying over their heads, and Roberts fired his one-twenty, three, four, five times in rapid succession, and the guns were suddenly silent. They could see men running there now, running and falling as they sought to escape to the flanks, and then the sixties opened up and bracketed them, and Roberts eased the big mortar over again and laid down a steady barrage behind them.

Up on the hill, Bramble had left the shelter and was stretched out on the ground, his glasses to his eyes. Duyvel was beside him, and Bramble said: 'Hold off the Browning, the survivors are making for the forest where the Indians are.'

'Ahmed Idriss is there,' Duyvel said. 'Idriss and all the archers, in between them.'

'Good. Left flank seems to be holding.'

'Not holding, sir. Wiped out.'

Bramble was swinging the glasses over. 'Two teams of machine-gunners moving into the gorge, Duyvel, you'd better stop them, fast.'

Duyvel spoke again: 'Carlo? Immediately to your left, range about four hundred yards, two machine-guns, can you see them?'

The elderly Carlo's voice was clear over the radio: 'I see them. A Hotchkiss and a Maxim, you want me to do something about them.'

Duyvel saw that he had opened fire almost before he stopped speaking, and the two guns went up in the burst of a single three-pound shell; it was fired from his 60mm. mortar, fitted with an under-size base plate, its weight cut to eighteen pounds, so that it could be used by one man as a hand-held weapon. Maximum range, eighteen hundred yards, maximum speed of operation, thirty-five rounds per minute, though the men of the Private Army were trained up to forty, or even forty-two.

And now, the survivors at the edge of the river were recovering from the initial surprise of the attack. They were brave and savage men, the *mestizos*, cruel and cunning and violent, but not lacking in courage. For some of them, a fight against heavy odds was the only kind of fight they believed in; how were they to know there were only a hundred-odd men against them?

But those hundred men had spent the night in well-trained silence, slinging the guns across the impossible gorge on ropes, digging in on the flanks around and behind them, setting up the deadly mortars which could reduce their thousands to a few score in a matter of minutes.

Santarem, the commander, was crawling painfully to where his leader, Juan Xira, had taken shelter at the first outbreak of murderous fire. He was dragging a shattered leg behind him, a Schmeisser machine-pistol in his hands, using it as an anchor to haul himself along. He rolled over on his back beside Xira, curled up there under a rock, and staring stolidly out into the forest. He said, furious: 'What happened, Juan? What happened?'

Xira shook his head, and said nothing. The shells were bursting all around them, constantly pounding, the shrapnel clipping through the heavy foliage, cutting it to shreds.

Santarem looked over to the flanks and said: 'And there's no way out, they've got us pinned down, nowhere to go . . .'

Xira turned his cold, glassy eyes on him. Santarem saw now that there was a livid wound at the side of his neck, a long fresh scar from the nape to the lobe of the ear. Three shells landed in close succession close behind them, ten feet on the other side of their protective boulders; he heard the sandstone shatter.

He felt the hatred in those cold eyes, and it shocked him. He saw Jugasto, the leader of the Fifth Commando, running, bent low, and he was grinning, a wide, sardonic grin; there was no amusement in it.

Santarem said sharply, re-establishing the authority he felt he was losing: 'Well?'

Jugasto pointed: 'Every one of those hills out there, it's thick with them. They must have ten thousand men around us, more in the forest.'

Santarem said heavily: 'Bring in the Indians.'

Jugasto spat; there was blood in the saliva. He said: 'Two things. First of all, the Indians won't come out of their jungle, we always knew that, and the enemy doesn't look like beating through to them, they're staying put in those hills, and why shouldn't they, they've got us in the bottom of a barrel. And secondly, we can't get to the Indians. They have four, five, six hundred archers along the flank of the forest . . .'

'Archers!'

'Bowmen.' He held out a single arrow, and said: 'Look at that, that's cedar, and the fletching is grey-goose feather, that's a very high class shaft. And the Brazilian army doesn't use archers, so who the hell is it out there, can you tell me that?'

Xira's eyes were still on him, and the violence in Jugasto's voice terrified him. He said: 'Goddammit, get a couple of hundred men together, a raiding force, break through to the Indians, do I have to tell you your job?'

'A couple of hundred men?' Jugasto's voice was very low now. He said slowly: 'Less than an hour ago, we had seven thousand two hundred and ten effectives. You know what the count is now? On this flank, we're down to under three hundred, and the shells are still pounding us, and over on the other flank . . . I can't even get to them, but they had the heavy guns, and a one-twenty mortar has been pounding them for thirty-five minutes, I doubt if there are ten men left alive over there. How come they got on the hills above us, can you tell me that? What happened to the probing force, it ought to be behind them now, in the gorge, and it isn't, can you answer me that too? You're the

Commander, Santarem. Tell me what's gone wrong?'

Xira said softly: 'Tell me too, Santarem.'

As Santarem blustered, he saw Xira pull out his revolver, a British Enfield .38. He flipped open the cylinder, looked at it, and said: 'Three bullets left . . . '

Jugasto shook his head. He said: 'Save them, Juan, he's not worth the price of a bullet, even when they're free.'

Santarem swung up his Schmeisser, but the movement of Jugasto's arm was so fast he did not see the flash of the blade, and then the knife was in his stomach and ripping upwards to the chest, not coming out till the tip of it went through the throat, bottom to top, and flicked at the jaw-bone. His teeth had bitten through his tongue when he died, and he lay there with his eyes open and still staring.

Xira looked at Jugasto and nodded slowly. 'Can we get to the helicopter?'

'We can try.'

'A thousand pounds of high explosive in its belly, it's not much but . . . '

There was pleasure in Jugasto's wide grin now. 'Bombs?'

'Four two hundred and fifty-pound naval bombs.'

'There, then . . . ' Jugasto parted the foliage with a bleeding hand, and pointed. He said: 'Less than a mile, near the top of the hill, that's where they've got a command post. Take these, take a look.'

He handed over his binoculars, and Xira stared out and said: 'I see nothing.'

'The wild begonias.'

'Nothing.'

'You see the fallen papaya tree?'

'I see it.'

'A runner went in under it ten minutes ago.'

Xira said sourly: 'That makes it a command post?'

'The only site from which the whole of the battle is visible, yes, that makes it a command post.'

'Who are they, Jugasto?'

'Does it matter who they are? The whole world's our enemy, Xira, isn't it? We'll drop our bombs on them, and then . . . '

'Then?'

'We have enough fuel to take us to Manaus.'

'And then?'

Jugasto shrugged; 'Chile, Cuba, Algeria. Or Venezuela, if you

139

like. Plenty of places left in the world where we can stir up a revolution, you and I.'

'Which way?'

'Through here.'

The wounded were still screaming, the shells still pounding, as they crawled together along a track that had been made for them, during the night, by a jaguar.

Duyvel said, the glasses to his eyes: 'Eight, ten, maybe twelve of their machine-guns still firing.'

Bramble nodded: 'The Brownings, then. Keep the fire to one side, the left, I'd say. If they want to cut and run now, let's give them the chance. They'll never worry anyone again.'

Duyvel gave the order into his radio, and the heavy .50 M2s opened up, a sustained and steady barrage that cut from the edge of the gorge to the jungle, stopping at the beginnings of the forest where the hordes of the Indians were waiting – if they were still there; would they have followed Blackman back to their village? – and then moving swiftly back again.

Paul Tobin was squatting at the edge of the camouflage, a mass of creeping lantana over his shoulders, staring down on to the swamp and the plain. He said: 'Helicopter taking off.'

They watched it, the three of them, and Paul said a moment later: 'Coming our way, right overhead, unless he changes course. Has he seen us, do you think?'

Bramble said: 'Let's not run that risk. You take it Paul. Use the PIAT, that's a Naval helicopter, armored underneath.'

Paul said: 'I've got it.' He rolled over and grimaced at the sudden pain in his shoulder, and said, startled: 'My God, I forgot, I've got a piece of shrapnel under my shoulderblade . . .'

'Can you handle it?'

'I can handle it.'

He was using full charge now, the five-pound projectile that would blow a medium-sized tank to pieces with a single hit. He held the helicopter in his sights, and waited, the four-finned shell resting in the forward container. Edgars had modified the fins too, giving them a twelve-degree sweep for added range, and the nose was altered too, a deep-grooved screw-thread running round it for added penetration.

Duyvel was easing himself closer, a better point of vantage, and Paul said: 'Keep out of the way of the recoil, Captain, or you'll be a lieutenant tomorrow. A dead lieutenant.' The recoil of the increased-velocity shell could blast a hole in a man's stomach big enough to crawl through.

Bramble said: 'Four thousand feet on the range-finder. Yes, he's coming right at us. Three thousand five hundred, three thousand . . . twenty-five . . . twenty . . . my God, he's diving on us . . .'

Paul fired the PIAT.

He felt the tremendous recoil burn its way into the shrubbery and the rocks behind him, felt the heat of it bounce back off the soil, and the thought came to him quickly: 'My God, what did Edgars put in that damn thing . . . ? He dived for cover as the shell hit the hard underside of the helicopter, rolled over on his back to see it burst into flames, and then . . . Then, a massive explosion tore it into a thousand fragments that went flying through the hot blue sky and crashed into the ground all over the mountain.

And, with the roar of the explosion, the guns and the mortars fell silent, and there was only the quiet of the humid, steaming, countryside again.

Duyvel looked at Major Bramble. The Major nodded: 'All units withdraw. Rendezvous, nine point three miles up the river, the launches are waiting to take them to Xingu.'

He turned to Paul: 'Handing over command again, Major. It's over.'

They sat round the bamboo table in the little hut that looked across the wild pampas grass of the Mato Grosso; Colonel Tobin, his son Paul, and Major Bramble, Rick Meyers, and Betty de Haas with her now redundant maps. Pamela Charles, wearing her see-through gold-link dress now, her current favorite for after-dark, was bringing them the polished teak tray with the glasses, the ice, and the Colonel's bottle of Irish. The light of the oil-lamps was warm and comforting, the night breeze blowing cool over the open verandah.

The Colonel said: 'Casualties?'

'Three men dead, eleven wounded, four of them for hospi-talisation,' Paul said. 'Alaric in charge of the casualties, with Ramatul Singh and two nurses we hired in Manaus.'

'And Rio?'

Rick Meyers shuffled his papers. 'The Brazilian army is back on the job, removing explosive charges all over town. The Xirista movement is dead.'

'And there's one more thing, isn't there?'

Meyers smiled: 'Colonel Itaguari? Yes, he's been arrested by the

141

Military Police. In exchange for clemency, which means a long time in jail, he's agreed to give the authorities a list of every man known to be on the Death Squads. There'll be some sweeping changes at the Defense Ministry, and at Police Headquarters.'

'And the Minister?'

The smile broadened: 'The Minister is currently doing his level best to claim credit for the entire operation.'

'Good. Let him have it. Paul . . . my report?'

'Can I have a couple of days?'

'No. I'm leaving for London tomorrow, have to see the Ambassador from the Congo. I need it before I leave.'

Paul nodded. 'All right, then we'll have Bramble prepare it. After all, it was his battle.'

'Agreed.' The Colonel said, slyly: 'Betty, perhaps you'd like to give him a hand . . . '

She was looking at Bramble, her face flushed. 'Of course, I'll be glad to.'

'Then that just about wraps it all up. Charles, will you pour us all a drink? I need the taste of Irish in my throat.'

The Colonel took his son's arm and they went out together on to the verandah, looking out across the moon-swept plain, the dark grasses tall and swaying slightly in the breeze, the distant mountains where the jungle began, a dark, dark purple, the round moon bright above them.

The Colonel said: 'And you, Paul . . . will you come back to London with me? We can take the Bellanca to Manaus, there's a Varig plane leaving at midday.'

'No. If you wouldn't mind.' He ran a hand through his tousled hair, and said: 'Some unfinished busines in Rio. A lady.'

'Ah, the lovely Estrella?'

'Estrella Cheleiros. If you can spare me, I thought we'd have a couple of weeks in Montevideo. There's a lot she has to forget.'

'So it's like that.'

'For the moment, at least, it's like that.'

They leaned on the railing and watched Major Bramble and Betty de Haas, an official-looking file of maps under her arm, as they walked towards the bungalow on the water's-edge. Rick Meyers had found a log to sit on by the bank of the stream, and was staring at nothing and brooding, thinking about the Ruachi Indians and their customs.

The Colonel sighed. He thumped his son on the shoulder where the pea-sized piece of shrapnel was lodged, and said gruffly:

'All right, Paul, I'll see you in London. Give me a call as soon as you get in. No doubt there'll be work to do.'

He went back inside. Pamela Charles was standing there, tall and slim and elegant, very poised and cool, the gold-link chain-work tight around her torso, intricately worked to follow the curves of her hips, her splendid breasts; the naked flesh beneath it was the color of ivory, smooth and demanding; she was the alabaster statue of an emperor's favorite *odalisque*.

He said, almost brusquely: 'Charles, let's go to your room. I need you.'

'Yes, sir.'

Paul stood on the verandah and watched them go, both of them with that strange, almost feline walk that was half-stealth, half-ease.

He came in and poured himself another drink, and went back out there to stare up at the stars and let the dark of the night close around him.

Over the endless pampas, the breezes were stirring gently; and everything was silent.

NEL BESTSELLERS

Crime

T013 332	CLOUDS OF WITNESS	Dorothy L. Sayers	40p
T016 307	THE UNPLEASANTNESS AT THE BELLONA CLUB	Dorothy L. Sayers	40p
W003 011	GAUDY NIGHT	Dorothy L. Sayers	40p
T015 556	MURDER MUST ADVERTISE	Dorothy L. Sayers	40p

Fiction

T013 944	CRUSADER'S TOMB	A. J. Cronin	60p
T013 936	THE JUDAS TREE	A. J. Cronin	50p
T012 271	THE WARSAW DOCUMENT	Adam Hall	40p
T012 778	QUEEN IN DANGER	Adam Hal!	30p
T009 769	THE HARRAD EXPERIMENT	Robert H. Rimmer	40p
T013 820	THE DREAM MERCHANTS	Harold Robbins	75p
T012 255	THE CARPETBAGGERS	Harold Robbins	80p
T016 560	WHERE LOVE HAS GONE	Harold Robbins	75p
T013 707	THE ADVENTURERS	Harold Robbins	80p
T006 743	THE INHERITORS	Harold Robbins	60p
T009 467	STILETTO	Harold Robbins	30p
T015 289	NEVER LEAVE ME	Harold Robbins	40p
T016 579	NEVER LOVE A STRANGER	Harold Robbins	75p
T011 798	A STONE FOR DANNY FISHER	Harold Robbins	60p
T015 874	79 PARK AVENUE	Harold Robbins	60p
T011 461	THE BETSY	Harold Robbins	75p
T010 201	RICH MAN, POOR MAN	Irwin Shaw	80p
T009 718	THE THREE SIRENS	Irving Wallace	75p

Historical

T009 750	THE WARWICK HEIRESS	Margaret Abbey	30p
T013 731	KNIGHT WITH ARMOUR	Alfred Duggan	40p
T009 734	RICHMOND AND ELIZABETH	Branda Honeyman	30p
T014 649	FAIROAKS	Frank Yerby	50p

Science Fiction

T014 347	SPACE RANGER	Isaac Asimov	30p
T016 900	STRANGER IN A STRANGE LAND	Robert Heinlein	75p
T011 534	I WILL FEAR NO EVIL	Robert Heinlein	75p
T011 844	DUNE	Frank Herbert	75p
T012 298	DUNE MESSIAH	Frank Herbert	40p

War

T009 890	THE K BOATS	Don Everitt	30p
T013 324	THE GOOD SHEPHERD	C. S. Forester	35p
W002 484	THE FLEET THAT HAD TO DIE	Richard Hough	25p
T011 755	TRAWLERS GO TO WAR	Lund & Ludlam	40p

Western

T017 001	EDGE: No. 4: KILLER'S BREED	George Gilman	30p
T016 536	EDGE: No. 5: BLOOD ON SILVER	George Gilman	30p
T013 774	EDGE: No. 6: THE BLUE, THE GREY AND THE RED	George Gilman	25p

General

T011 763	SEX MANNERS FOR MEN	Robert Chartham	30p
W002 531	SEX MANNERS FOR ADVANCED LOVERS	Robert Chartham	25p
T010 732	THE SENSUOUS COUPLE	Dr. 'C'	25p

NEL P.O. BOX 11 FALMOUTH, CORNWALL

Please send cheque or postal order. Allow 6p per book to cover postage and packing.

Name ....

Address...

....

Title ....
(APRIL)